Who's Been Stealing Grandpa's Fish?

WHO'S BEEN STEALING GRANDPA'S FISH?

Library of Congress Control Number: 2017939993
ISBN: 978-1-944962-40-1 (paperback)

Secant Publishing, LLC
P.O. Box 79
Salisbury, MD 21803

www.secantpublishing.com

Who's Been Stealing Grandpa's Fish?

SUSAN YARUTA-YOUNG

SECANT PUBLISHING

To my grandfather:

Simeon Yaruta Sr. (July 1888–November 1966),
Russian-born, immigrant to America (1907),
who loved flowers, forests, and landscaping.

In the 1920s, using money he'd saved, he bought a small
farm in what is now called Caves Valley, composed of
woodlands and fields. Here he built a house for my
grandmother, Minnie,and their two children: my dad,
Simeon Jr., and my Aunt Mar.

Introduction

Imagine living in a place where every season children, teens, young adults, grownups visited as if it were a state or national park. A place filled with wild rushing streams, bubbling springs, ponds; fields to venture through; trees to explore, hide in low boughs, climb, or swing from. A world where you could wander from sunrise until sunset in grassy fields, under shady bushes, and discover many adventures on forest trails. Land where everywhere, wild creatures covered in feathers, fur, silky skin, and/or scales hid in burrows, stream shallows, shadowy barns, marshy meadows, watching you as you looked for them.

Imagine discovering your home, where you spent days, evenings, nights, playing, exploring, learning, experiencing the world around you . . . was a world your grandfather had learned from, where your mom was shown secrets of deep earth. Imagine believing the place where you lived was "nothing special" until wildlife encounters suddenly made you realize differently.

The Property where Max and Charles lived was just such a place. The book you are about to read describes the day they discovered many special secrets. This day in May they realized their family's land was a wonder-filled world where ancient woodland stories were heard, memorized, recited, passed down through generations from parent to child, where new stories waited to begin.

Excerpt from Max's Writing Journal: 'Alliteration' Words Describing Home

Waking, walking, wandering, wondering
wild woodlands whisper wishes, warnings.

Still springs suddenly spiral,
streams slushing, splashing, swishing, surging;
slithering slippery, silent, slick,
sleek, salamanders seek safe sheltered sleep;
sprinkling sun splinters streak sunrise, sunset.

Adventures advance
as ants attacking anything.

Running, rushing, rolling, revolving,
rescuing, reaching.

Fir forest.
Faint flickering, flash,
flipping, fins forging, fingerlings,
fishing fish.

Chapter 1

Breakfast with Grandparents and Talk of a 'Murder'

At 6:08 a.m., Saturday, May 1, 1985, Max, age eleven, and his eight-year-old brother Charles were wide awake. They were watching streams of sunrise fill their room with shades of pink, gold, and blue light. Who could sleep when a huge glowing show covered the sky canvas and, closer, swirly streaks and puff clouds were constantly changing into new shapes?

"What a sunrise," Max said, stretching. "Think of the old saying: 'Red skies in the morning, sailors' warning. Red skies at night, sailors' delight.' Looks like it might be an interesting day."

Second by second outside, and their room, became brighter and brighter.

Then Charles said, "This is all very nice, but my stomach is empty. It's growling. And you can bet breakfast here won't be until 8. Mom and Fred like to sleep in on Saturdays."

"So what do you want to do, genius?" Max yawned.

"Grandma and Grandpa have breakfast *every* morning all fixed by 6:30."

"You want to crash their quiet and have a hearty meal?" Max asked. He threw off the single sheet, sat up, and dangled his two long feet over the upper bunk.

"Yeah. Why not? They'll understand. I'm starved. Last night's early dinner and early to bed has me, not wealthy, but wise enough to know that to be healthy, my tummy needs filling. And, anyway, I'm wide-awake hungry."

"Me too. OK, let's do it." Max pushed off and landed into the thick, fake-fur polar bear rug.

Charles waited for Max's landing before rolling from the bottom bunk. He turtle-crawled to a clothes dresser, yanked open the bottom drawer, and tugged free shorts and a T-shirt. He loved May in Maryland; dressing took minutes.

By 6:20 both boys had washed their faces, done tooth scrubs, were dressed, and were exiting their bedroom. They crept down the hall, slipped out the back door, did a "congrats" high-five, then bolted in a "who can run the fastest" race through the seven-acre field which separated their cedar-shake Cape Cod home from their grandparents' sprawling farmhouse.

The field's tall grass was cool and thick with dew. Long green stems swished against their legs, soft, dry tops tickled in an itchy sort of way. Closer to the grove of big trees where their grandparents' house was, grass was short, a carpet of green, thick in clover, mixed with soft, golf course-like grasses. It was comfy to their feet. From late April until fall, Grandpa mowed it often, stirring tiny insects from hiding places into the air. Just a few days ago, once again, he'd been followed by a flock of barn swallows swooping down to snatch their flying meals. They nested every year in the garage/pony shed, across the driveway from the farmhouse.

At 6:28 exactly, the boys entered the backyard. Yappy, Grandpa's beagle, was sitting in his favorite place: the flat roof of his dog house. He began to bay. Max raced to Yappy, giving him the necessary head pat and behind-the-ears scratch. "I must wash hands before breakfast. Phew! Yappy, you sure do smell."

Yappy, who ignored any and all criticism, licked Max's face. He was content having attention. He curled into a brown-black-white donut shape and returned to his nap.

Charles checked his "multi-do this/do that" wristwatch, signaled Max it was almost time. Exactly at 6:30 both boys stood side-by-side on their grandparents' cement back porch.

"One. Two. Three. Knock!"

Knuckles of two right hands did the "tap-do-de-tap-tap, tap-tap" rhythm for knocking their grandfather had taught them when they were small.

Within seconds, Fitzgerald — F. Scott or Fitz for short — was at the screen door, pushing her black nose against the wire and moaning softly. She was Grandma's favorite, a tri-colored, three-year-old English setter, the runt of a litter of twelve pups. Grandpa had brought her home one night for Grandma to bottle feed. Using a special recipe, the pup was fed every two hours until she was big enough to eat on her own. Charles, not knowing she was not a he, named her after the famous writer. Grandpa and Grandma liked the name and kept it even though her name confused company who had never been to the house before.

Seconds after Fitz's arrival at the screen door, Grandma appeared, wiping her hands on a dish rag and pretending to look shocked.

"Oh, my goodness! Who do we have here?" she laughed, opening the door.

"We're the Wilderness Boys, and we're very hungry for breakfast, Grandma," Max said.

"Well, come in! Come in!" she said. "Grandpa, look who we have here! Two Wilderness Boys arrived for breakfast. Imagine, company at 6:30."

"Hmm?" Their grandfather turned his head to see. He stood shaving with a barber-style straight razor. Between swipes with the sharp blade, he watched a downy woodpecker and a nuthatch take turns pecking suet from a feeder, hanging from an oak tree limb outside the window.

"Max and Charles are hungry for breakfast," Grandma told Grandpa. She turned to the boys. "Your mom and Fred sleeping in, I guess?"

"Sleeping late? Wasting the prettiest part of the day, sunrise," Grandpa said. He made a final swipe from his chest bone, over his Adam's apple, up to his chin. He wiped Ivory soap off the razor with his pocket handkerchief, then returned the razor to the highest cabinet shelf. He picked up the coffee mug, which was filled with melted soap and a badger hair shaving brush, and carried it to the kitchen sink. He'd wash it later. He turned on the faucet, splashed water on his tanned cheeks, wiped his face dry on the back of his shirt sleeve, then turned to the boys. He was done in less time than it takes to count to ten.

The boys patted Fitz and watched their Grandpa. *'What a pro at barber-style shaving,'* Max thought.

"So, you boys want a real Saturday breakfast while the morning is still young. Good for you," he said. He patted both boys on the tops of their floppy, uncombed hair.

"What sounds good?" Grandma asked. "I was going to fix bacon and eggs, cinnamon toast from the Amish market, juice, and coffee."

"All of it, Grandma . . . minus the coffee," Charles said.

"But hot tea in a saucer with honey from your beehives would be great," Max added.

"Coming right up," Grandma said. "You can set yourselves places at the table. Grandpa, we need extra bacon cut from the slab."

"As ordered," he said. He straightened his khaki-colored work shirt, pushed its tail back into khaki work pants, and adjusted his pale-green with tan-striped suspenders. "One of you boys want to help?"

"I'll set the table. Charles, go help Grandpa," Max said. He knew what job he wanted. And he knew it would seem boring to Charles, but then his younger brother wasn't clued in to all the kitchen secrets. It was the job of an older brother to allow a little brother fun stuff once in a while. Besides, by setting the table, Max had access to Grandma's stack of china and could find her spinning plate, the plate he wanted his breakfast on. *A win-win. Charles learns about how bacon is cut from a slab and I get the best plate Grandma has,'* Max thought.

"Come on, boy," Grandpa said to Charles, opening the door to the glassed-in back porch. "Duck under my arm then make a left. Stop at the bench. No, Fitzgerald, I don't need your help on this project," Grandpa said, pushing the dog back and closing the kitchen door.

Fitz whined.

"Come here, sweetie," Grandma cooed. "Go and rest on your blanket like a good girl while we have breakfast. There'll be plenty of goodies for you and Yappy if you're good."

Fitz sighed but did as Grandma said. She circled three times before nestling down on her pink blanket. She put her long nose between front paws, closed her eyes, and, moments later, was snoring.

Charles followed Grandpa's directions and found the bench where a large package sat, wrapped in butcher paper and tied with a peppermint-like, red-and-white string. The package looked like a floppy box.

"Here's the bacon," Grandpa said.

"There?" Charles asked. He'd never seen bacon wrapped in white paper.

"Yes, sir, right in there. Pull the end of that string until the bow is gone. It's just like Christmas, except it's May."

Charles took the end of the string. He pulled until the

bow disappeared. He helped Grandpa unwrap, unwrap, and unwrap until a long, brown slab of smoked bacon was uncovered.

"Now," said Grandpa, taking a large carving knife from off a very high shelf, "we choose how thick we want each slice. We cut enough bacon for breakfast, then re-wrap in paper and put it away in the porch icebox where it will stay cool."

"Icebox?"

"Oops. I used the old-fashioned word for it. Can't seem to wrap my mind around using grand-sounding long words I didn't grow up using. You know: refrigerator. Do you know why I call it an icebox?"

Charles had heard his grandmother's story why, but now he could hear Grandpa's version.

"Why?"

"Well, a long time ago, when I was knee high to a groundhog . . ." he held out his arm measuring about two-and-a-half feet high.

Charles thought, *'I don't think I ever want to meet a groundhog that tall,'* but he didn't say anything.

". . . my folks had that." Grandpa pointed to the white painted cabinet. "It's a real icebox. Go and open it."

Charles did as he was told. He opened the longest door first. Inside, he saw shelves like those in an oven. Piled on them were Grandma's cleaning rags and her bag of clothespins for wash days.

"See the sides? What are they made of?" Grandpa asked.

"Looks like metal painted white."

"Close. Enamel over metal to keep things cold inside.

But we needed something else. We needed ice. Open the small bottom door on the left."

Charles looked. "No racks and it's not white enamel, just plain old metal, nothing special," he said. "Oh, and on the bottom there's a little hole."

"This is the place where large blocks of ice went."

"And the hole?" Charles asked.

"Where water dripped through when the ice melted."

"What a big mess!"

"Look outside, on the very bottom: see a board? Pull it up."

Charles pulled and suddenly saw through to the porch floor. "Grandpa?"

"Ha!" Grandpa laughed. "Well, in my day a big pan was kept behind that board, under the hole and caught all the water. The board you lifted kept it hidden, safe from dogs who might take a drink. We used the water for washing. In those days we lived the slogan 'waste not, want not.' It was during what is known now as 'The Great Depression.'"

Charles nodded. "We studied about it this year in history class."

"Good. Good for children to know about those hard times. In far back days, the Ice Man arrived in a truck, but before engines were invented, he came in a wooden wagon pulled by a work horse, sometimes two. The wagon, later truck, was where ice was stacked surrounded by wood shavings to keep it from melting, blocks and blocks of stacked ice. The Ice Man knew exactly what size blocks every person on his route needed to fit in their ice boxes. He'd carry in the block using big steel 'pincers.'

When it was cold — in the winter, late fall, and some cold springs — we didn't need the Ice Man. We could easily keep things cold on the porch. But come summer, the Ice Man made deliveries every few days. OK, Charles, so much for your 'Ice Age' history lesson for today. Let's cut bacon."

Charles watched as Grandpa sawed the knife blade through tough outer hide, through fat, through pink meat. He did it ten times. Bacon slices didn't fall but stood upright.

"Now I have to cut slices away from the bottom," he said. He knelt on both knees, angled the slab of bacon back and forth until it was to his liking, positioned his knife close to the thick hide and began cutting. As he cut, the slices tipped over on top of each other.

Charles counted them "1, 2, 3, 4, 5, 6, 7, 8, 9, 10."

Meanwhile, in the kitchen, Max washed Fitz-stinky hands, then began hunting for the spinning plate. He stood on Grandma's stepladder and opened the cabinet where she stacked her everyday dishes. Examining several for the special mark on the bottom of the plate, he found it. Next he took another plate, with the same design: yellow and blue flowers spilling from orange baskets, *'a plate for Charles which looks like mine.'* As he'd been taught by Grandma, he finished setting the table, placing the spinning plate where he always sat.

Grandma had her back turned away from him. She was cutting cinnamon bread to toast. As quietly as possible, Max tested the plate. He gave it a push. It spun in place. "Yes!" he said to himself. "Score!"

Breakfast was a feast. Grandma cooked the bacon until it was crispy and juicy. Poached eggs were fixed as the boys liked them best. Homemade butter dripped from spicy sweet cinnamon toast. Icy-cold orange juice wasn't watery, bitter, or too sweet. Tea in a saucer sweetened with chewy honeycomb taken from Grandpa's hives was a special treat.

Max expertly spun the special spinning plate: if he wanted eggs in front, one careful spin, there they were; another nudge, the plate turned to his pile of toast, stopping right below his nose. Fun.

After breakfast, Max cleared the table while Charles helped Grandpa feed the tropical fish. Before flaky food was flicked in to swimming mollies, orange swordfish, neon tetra, guppies, and miniature clown fish, all were calmly gliding back and forth on the bubbling waters. When "breakfast" was served, they rose to the surface in a wild rushing swirl, slapping splash drops against the tank glass. All the fish, except for the upside down one who was always tail up, nose down, belly rubbing the glass as it nibbled furry green slime with sucking open mouth, whipping long whiskers back and forth like the huge monster catfish found prowling in Alabama channels or roaming the Tennessee River.

Tall green plants decorated and protected tiny fish from bigger ones. Grandpa even had a special plastic "birthing and nursery" box where newborn fish were safe from others. The aquarium had mountains made of pebbles, several stone archways, and one stone bridge which Grandma had built. The bottom was covered in clean white and gray sand. Special lights made the aquarium bluish-green. The glowing aquarium bathed the dining room in a calming light; the humming motor and bubbling sounds, as air churned the water, made a soothing background sound. Looking through the glass into this watery world was like peering into the never-ending drama of water creatures.

Meanwhile, in the kitchen, Max, who had fed Grandpa's tropical fish three years longer than Charles, dried the dishes for Grandma.

"I must remember to give you the spinning plate when you come down again. It was Great-Grandma's, you know. She always said it was for lazy eaters. During family get-togethers at her house, my cousins and I, like you, always tried to sit where that spinning plate set. Your Uncle Mike once spun it so fast his green beans went flying across the table like torpedoes, landing on everybody's plates. Watching, your Great-Granddad said, 'Why, land's sake, Mammo, I think the young'uns have begun warfare! You best hurry and begin serving them blueberry pie you baked before cannons start firing!'" Grandma laughed at the memory.

"What were the cannons?" Max asked.

"Oh, heavens, child. I imagine he meant all nine of us cousins burping at once."

Max swallowed. Wow! Hard to imagine Grandma, his aunts and uncles having a burping battle at the dinner table.

The phone rang. It was the boys' mother.

"Yes, dear. Yes, they're here. Oh, no. No trouble. They

were hungry. We fed them full. We're having a good time. Now, stop fretting and don't you worry. Enjoy your Saturday with Fred and the baby. Ralph's asleep? I suspected. Well, best not to wake him."

Ralph was their older brother. He was old enough to date and stay out late on weekends and holidays, which he did. He had a lanky girlfriend Max and Charles called "Turkey Legs Toni" (a secret name they never dared say to anyone else, particularly Ralph). In code they referred to her as T. L. Toni, which might have translated as "Tender Loving Toni" to others.

Dishes dried, tropical fish fed, the boys followed Grandpa onto the cement porch to watch him trick the crows. They sat on the top step while Grandpa stood looking around the grove of oak trees. "Ah, there, I see one," he pointed to a black-feathered bird perched high on a limb. "Let's see what kind of excitement I can stir up." He lifted his head and made a deep rattling "caw-CAW-caw!"

Immediately the crow answered: "Caw? Caw?"

Grandpa returned with a series of low, high, higher, low again, emotional sounding caws.

Max, Charles, and Grandpa could see the crow ruffling his feathers, shifting from one foot to the other, stretching his neck, pointing his beak straight into the sky, then ruffle feathers again.

"He looks agitated," Max said.

"I imagine he might be," Grandpa answered. He cleared his throat, took a deep breath and: "Caaaw, Caaaaw, Caaaaaaaaw!"

The crow left the branch, and began circling, as if weaving a string in and out through the tops of the oak tree, cawing louder and louder.

Soon another crow arrived, followed by another and another.

"Getting a group together." Grandpa cackled his funny laugh. He repeated the same three caws, but this time faster, faster, and in different tones, as if he was more than one crow.

The boys and Grandpa watched as crows began gathering. Some acted surprised. It looked as if they were pulling mid-air skids and saying among themselves, 'Where is the crow we hear but don't see?' Did they want to aggressively get to him? Were they changing their minds? Maybe going after *that* crow was not a good idea.

Grandpa cawed again, deep in his throat: "Caw-Caw-Caaaaaaaw!" It was a scary, commanding sound. Max and Charles could feel and see goose bumps rising up and down their arms.

Immediately, all crows began flying away, a quickly formed feathered force retreating to a safer "fort." In less than a minute they were gone. The soft, pale, green leaves of May were still. Not one crow stayed. In a few more moments, songbirds began to sing.

"Guess I told 'em!" Grandpa said, laughing. He eased down onto the cement porch. He leaned against the shingled house walls. He rested his work-booted feet on steps below. "So, boys, we'll talk crow." He patted the porch for them to sit beside him, which they did.

"Yes, what just happened?" Max asked.

"Well, crows are mighty smart critters. Over years I've learned plenty from them. I had a couple as pets. They know how to steal. They steal pretty things, shiny things, and hide them in places, always the same places. My one crow, Woody Wilson, stole my mom's bracelet, necklace, a fork, and little things like paper clips and shiny bits of ribbon. I had a huge cage for him and in it I put a World War I helmet I'd been given. Every day I'd open his cage door and let him free so he could go and come, do whatever pleased him. About once a week I'd clean his cage, and it was then I'd find treasures he'd stolen."

"He sounds like he was a great pet," Max said.

"He was. But crows have a nasty side, too. Going way back to the 1500s, there are stories of crows going to battlefields and finding their meals . . ."

"Ugh, you mean eating left-behind food, right?" Charles asked.

"No, son, much worse."

"Dead soldiers," Max said, bunching up his body and scrunching his face.

"So folk stories tell," said Grandpa. He put his arm around Charles. He looked at Max covering his face with his hands. "OK, something a bit less grim, or maybe not . . . If a crow is hurt and dying, a member of his group will kill him so he doesn't suffer."

"Oh, OK," said Max, uncovering his face. "That's a bit better."

"Yes, humane. But then of course if they're hungry . . ." Grandpa stopped and let the boys' imagination take over.

"Yuck! Yuck!"

"OK. I'll stop there. But this is why a big group of crows has an interesting name. Do you know what it is?"

"Ah, lots of birds together are called a flock," Max said.

"True. And some people call a group of crows a flock, too. But the real name for a flock of crows is a 'murder'."

"Wow, really? In a grim way, that's cool!" Charles said.

"Yep, something you can tell people at school. Maybe even add to your teacher's vocabulary. One more fact, to wow your teachers, then we have morning chores to do."

"OK," said both boys.

"Well, in England, because of all the grim things crows did, some say tombstones are called 'Raven Stones'."

"Thanks, Grandpa. Now I have ideas for my next nature story assignment for English or science," said Max.

All three sat in silence listening to the quiet after all the cawing. They heard bird song, the rustle and rushing of the nearby stream as it swiftly went bubbling over tiny pink, white, and brown quartz stones. And closer, in the garage/pony shed and over by the field, they heard soft, haunting, melodious "ooo-ooo-ooo" calls of mourning doves; further away, "bob-bob-white" from quail. The yard around Grandma and Grandpa's house was more woods than lawn, and many different kinds of creatures could be found almost every day, all year round. Even on cold, dark winter days, when all was ice and snow, even then there were many sounds, and most especially when creatures needed extra help. Then Grandpa and Grandma spread cracked corn, peanuts, and different kinds of seeds, placing them in feeders around the house, yard, even in the fields.

Max, Charles, and Grandpa were still taking it easy listening when Grandma opened the door and Fitzgerald came bounding out, wagging her feathery tail across their faces, sitting down beside them, pawing for a "give me a shake," licking ears and necks as if they were her puppies and they needed a bath.

"OK, stop, stop! That tickles, Fitz," Charles said through his giggles. Grandpa gave an explosive "Ha!" laugh.

"OK, gentlemen, time for chores," said Grandma. She was standing behind them holding two white plastic buckets.

Chapter 2

Feeding the 'Piranhas' (Alias Trout)

"OK, fellas, feeding time. I know about 1,500 little brookies who must be getting rather FINicky since their breakfast is later than usual," Grandpa said. He wrapped his fingers around the wire handle of a white bucket.

"I'll get the other," Max said.

"Nice when company helps," Grandma said. She handed it to him.

"Can I help, too?" Charles asked in his "I'm feeling-left-out" voice.

"Indeed you can!" Grandma gave him two empty tin cans.

Once upon a time these old cans had held condensed soup. Most days Grandma made all the meals "from scratch," but when Grandpa's surprise-visit friends stayed for lunch or dinner, she moved into her most creative gear, making meals feeding three, four, five or more, all within minutes. Lunch was always served between 11:30 a.m. and noon or, as Grandpa would say, "the chow-down hour." It was under these stressful times Grandma added canned extras to her homemade broths, soups, and stews. Grandma and Grandpa always recycled. Clean used soup cans were useful in many ways, including scooping up and flinging fish chow to hungry trout.

Meanwhile, energized and ready to take on the world, Fitz ran over to Yappy. The two began their morning doggy play while Grandma kept watch over them. As it was spring and rabbits were nesting, Yappy was leashed or tied. The time for young beagles to chase rabbits was in the fall and winter months.

Grandpa and Max carried the white buckets full of Purina Trout Chow. Charles held a tin can in each hand and tapped them together: a marching rhythm.

Leaving the back cement porch, they ducked under drying bed sheets and work clothes Grandma had hung on the clothesline. The lines formed a triangle, and the hanging clothes curtained off the backyard. It looked like a private room or a little backstage area for nature's theatre.

"Nothing like moonbeam-dried bedclothes," Grandma often said. "Makes sleeping more restful. Moonbeams bring sweet dreams. When you wear moonbeam-dried clothes, your day will always be special."

The boys didn't know if this was an old adage or one of Grandma's "wisdom sayings," as Grandpa sometimes called them. They knew their mom believed in using moonbeams to dry what she hung on the clothesline. She liked to hang their play clothes outside on full-moon nights when she was on vacation. But since the arrival of baby Carrie, all clothes went into the washer and dryer. Washing for six ages — one, eight, eleven, seventeen, and two adults — sometimes made their home sound like a commercial laundry with machines humming all day long. Until Carrie grew bigger, their mom didn't have the energy or time for moonbeam clothes.

After leaving the backyard, Max, Charles, and Grandpa walked a path to the stream. On their way they passed the springhouse. It didn't look like a real house, maybe a playhouse sunken into the ground, only ten inches high with a flat roof which was six-feet square. To Max and Charles, it was really a miniature stage where they'd performed when they were smaller. The roof of the spring house was a stage for children under one-hundred pounds. When Charles and Max performed, Grandpa told everyone who came to visit, "Meet my actor grandsons. They're wise and lean growing up as busy workers on this small farm."

Before their grandparents' house had refrigerators, their great-grandparents placed perishables like milk and eggs in glass jars or clean crocks and sunk them into icy cold spring water. Now, the pure, clean water was pumped into the house for drinking.

After the springhouse, the slate stone path narrowed until it was only one-person wide. On one side a little steam trickled. On the other side, thick evergreen trees grew. In early spring, hundreds of jonquils, daffodils, and narcissus bloomed. Here the ground was damp, and in some places, marshy. Grandpa said if anyone walked in there and stepped down too hard, a new spring would emerge. The boys believed him. They were also afraid of possible "quicksand" but didn't dare mention it to Grandma, Grandpa or any grownup. They just stayed on the firmer ground.

Grandpa had taught the boys how to look for many creatures living in flowing, spring-fed streams. Crayfish and minnows, yes, but there were also the caddish flies, and when the weather was warm, both boys searched for these tiny, unique creatures.

"You boys have your eyes 'peeled back' so you can find the larvae home of a caddish fly?" Grandpa asked.

"We're looking Grandpa," Max said. He stopped walking and knelt by the shallow stream.

"Me too," said Charles, doing the same.

Grandpa put down the white bucket. He stepped so he had one foot on each side of the narrow stream. He bent and looked. In a moment he slyly said, "I see one. Can you?"

Both boys looked but didn't see.

Grandpa picked up a little stick and pointed to a place in the stream.

Max saw. He reached in and carefully picked it up.

"Anyone home?" Grandpa asked.

"I'm not sure," Max said.

Grandpa jumped so both of his feet were together on one side of the stream. He reached out.

Max placed what he'd found into Grandpa's palm.

"Good job! Yes, this is a caddish larvae home. Or it was. Looks like now it is vacant. See? It looks like a tiny telescope."

Grandpa told the boys all about the caddish fly. How it had a very short lifespan (as May flies and other flying insects do), but unlike others it had a long life in the larvae homes it made. Most curious of all, these tiny creatures built their shelters using tiny stones. "Some insects will make homes out of leaves and twigs, but caddish use real sand."

And if that wasn't amazing enough, they made tiny nets to gather pieces of plants to eat during their years in the larvae stage. "They're like freshwater farmers," Grandpa told them.

Finding a caddish larvae shelter or "home" was always a great find, but after the boys examined it, they both knew it must be returned to the stream. "It is best to let Mother Nature recycle all things we find," Grandpa said.

On the other side of the path, thick evergreen trees grew, making a shady place all year round. It was in this area, in the stream, a dam was built for Trout Pool #1. The pool was long and narrow, lined with cinder blocks. It ended with a second dam, exactly like the first. On the other side of this dam was Trout Pool #2. Beyond the trout pools, the stream divided into a little stream and a Big Spring.

The trout hatchery was built when Max was three months old. Grandpa had held him on his lap and supervised the building by members of the Maryland Fly Anglers, a fly-fishing club Grandpa helped form years before. Max loved to show pictures of Grandpa holding him. He enjoyed saying, "Yep, I was the assistant supervisor of this trout hatchery project."

The fishing friends built wooden frames, which looked like extra big screen doors, but instead of metal mesh were covered in chicken wire. They were simply called "screens." These screens were to protect trout from nocturnal visitors with a sweet tooth for fresh young fish. Highest on that bad boy list were raccoons.

"Give me a hand," Grandpa said. Together the boys helped lift and slide the screens to one side, one at a time.

"That's better."

Now they could see the mirror-still surface of the trout pools. Looking down through the clear water, they saw long, shadowy, undulating figures moving between one dam and the other.

"Well, we'd better feed these fine, fierce, fishy fiends," Grandpa said.

Max and Charles looked at each other knowingly. Grandpa was a real whiz when it came to alliteration, a fancy name for tongue-twisters.

"Let the morning feasting begin," Max announced.

Grandpa held one white bucket. Max put his down. Charles gave Max a can and they each dipped into one bucket, filling their cans half-full of trout chow.

"One, two, three, all together now."

They tossed the chow onto the still water of Pool #1.

Instantly the quiet brook trout became piranhas.

Well, actually, no. The trout only *acted* like piranhas. The calm water became rough with trout lunging after chow.

Big, hungry, beautiful brook trout — which moments ago had been sliding silently, fins barely stirring the quiet pool — were now in a feeding frenzy. The water became wavy, wild, as fish surfaced, crowding, jockeying for position, bodies knocking into each other, eyes wild, noses up, mouths opening wide and clamping shut . . . all after the chow.

"Like a Tarzan movie," Grandpa said. He always said the same thing.

When they first heard Grandpa make the comparison, Max and Charles didn't understand. Who's Tarzan? What were piranha fish? How were Grandpa's trout like piranhas?

Then one afternoon their mom rented a VHS of an old black-and-white Tarzan movie. Watching it, they saw scary scenes: bad guys waded into waters where they should not have gone and were attacked by piranhas. After watching the Tarzan movie, Charles and Max knew they were not nice fish.

Quickly the pellets they had cast onto the water were gone, but trout continued their search. As the first of the feed disappeared, Grandpa nudged: "Throw them another round."

"One, two, three. Toss!" Again the boys threw smelly pellets into the water. Again bodies crested, noses bumped, some lunged into the air, diving down, fin-to-fin. The wild waters of the pool became rougher, white-water churning, as the fish aggressively fought each other for food.

A third round was thrown and even the least aggressive trout gulped a morning repast.

One white plastic bucket empty. Another to go.

Grandpa led the way up the narrow path to Trout Pool #2.

Charles called out: "One, two, three, toss the feed!" Quiet water rough and wavy with a feeding frenzy. Two more tosses were needed here, too. The trout in #2 were just as hungry.

The second white bucket was nearly empty.

"OK, boys," Grandpa said. "Time to put down the buckets and enjoy the world of the Big Spring."

Max and Charles followed Grandpa to what looked like a small frog pond, but was, in fact, the Big Spring. Here the water was icy cold, clear, clean. When they looked in, they could see the bottom and all the creatures on it.

Around the Big Spring grew different flavors of mint: peppermint, spearmint, orange mint. On one side, a small stream fed into the Little Spring, and it was in this stream Grandpa urged Max and Charles to go and look at the thick crop of watercress, all sizes and shapes.

"Try the tiniest little pale-green leaves first," he said.

Max and Charles lay down on their bellies in thick green grass and reached in. At first they tried plucking little green leaves, but they were small and both boys began pulling up white tangles of root with tiny leaves on top.

"That's OK," Grandpa said. "Plenty of watercress. What does it taste like?"

Charles was first. He put the entire plant in his mouth and began to chew. He chewed and chewed. He was quiet a long time, which was very unlike Charles.

Watching his suddenly silent, chewing younger brother,

Max decided he'd best try the small watercress plant himself. His popped it in his mouth. He chewed and chewed and chewed.

"Well," said Grandpa.

"Well, it really doesn't taste like much. It sort of tastes like chewy water," Max said.

"Charles?"

"Yep, I agree with Max. I feel like I'm chewing water. Very, chewy water."

"Correct. That's because it's a young plant. Now, go for bigger leaves, the size of clover. Then tell me what those taste like."

The boys each rolled over and over in the thick grass until they reached a large patch of dark green, larger-leaf cress. These were even harder to pick.

"I wish I had scissors. I bet I could cut the cress with scissors," Max said.

"Here," Grandpa said. He pulled a pen knife from his pants pocket. Next he opened out the larger blade and handed the knife to Max, handle first. "I think this is sharp enough to cut what you need. Careful, I just sharpened it. It's sharp as my razor. Respect it."

"I will," said Max, gritting his teeth. He held the little penknife carefully, as Grandpa had taught him when he was about Charles age. He pulled several large watercress plants from the spring fed stream. In one hand he held the plant; with the knife in his other, he sawed white roots free from green stems and leaves.

"Here, Grandpa," he handed the knife back, handle first, as he'd been taught. Grandpa wiped the blade dry on his pants cuff, pushed the blade back in place, and returned it to his pocket.

Meanwhile, Max gave Charles some of the more-mature watercress leaves.

The larger cress burned their mouths as they chewed.

"My mouth is on fire! Smoke must be coming out of my ears!" Charles gasped. He spat and spat again, trying to get all of the watercress out of his mouth. Then he dropped his face into the spring water and drank.

"Yeah, Charles, I saw the fire," Max said. "I saw flames shoot out of your nose! It was like you'd turned into a dragon!"

Grandpa started to laugh his deep, caw-like laugh. "That's OK, Charles. Old Max had the same reaction back when he was your age. Now, yank up a few more of the peppery plants, about two each. Grandma has lunch plans for them. Here, Max, rinse out this empty chow bucket in the spring. Get it as clean as you can. We'll use it for hauling the cress back with us."

Meanwhile, Charles was slurping great mouthfuls of water and spitting it out. Max went to rinse out the bucket. Grandpa sat in the tall grass by the Big Spring.

Then Fitz arrived. She flopped beside Grandpa, placed her head on his tummy. She closed her eyes and immediately began to doze. She was entering mid-snore when her nose began twitching, eyes zipped open, lips pulled back into a doggie grin: she'd noticed Charles, who was pulling his wet face and hair out of the stream. Immediately she sprang up, went to him and began grooming his hair, ears and face with her tongue.

"Fitz, stop! That tickles. Fitz!" Charles said, giggling, wiggling, rolling over and burying his face in the lush grass as Fitz continued washing him.

Max looked up and laughed. Grandpa joined in.

"It's not fun-un-uny," Charles said. His words were blurred by the green lush grass.

"OK, Fitz. OK, girl, enough," Grandpa said. "Come here, Fitzgerald! Come!"

Fitz gave Charles a final ear lick and went to Grandpa. She curled near, laid her head on his legs, gave a big sigh, closed her eyes, and in seconds was asleep again.

"I guess playing with Yappy wore her out," Grandpa said.

The boys regrouped beside Grandpa.

"OK, enough watercress for now. Time to cleanse your palates. Look! See heavy grass growing in thick bunches? It's there right between where you're sitting and the Big Spring. Look sharp, there's a nice patch of peppermint hidden in the long grass. Enjoy," Grandpa said, pointing to the mint.

"That's better," Charles said.

"Yum," said Max.

"Try different leaves. Some is peppermint, some spearmint. Some tastes a bit like orange. Grandma will want peppermint. She likes to put it in iced tea."

"Yum."

"Southern-style sweet tea, too."

"Yum."

"Southern Style sweet tea with mint."

"Yummy."

Max and Charles knew Grandma's iced tea with mint tasted like no tea they'd ever had. It was the best. And so was her lemonade, which she also served with sprigs of fresh mint.

The Big Spring was where Grandpa kept his special "babies" selected from the 1,200-to-1,500 fingerling trout he raised every year. His favorite was the brook trout, or what he liked to call "brookies."

Every fall, a large truck arrived to deliver the three-inch fingerlings. Weekends before this annual due date, fishing club members and other helpers prepared the trout pools. They raked the stream bed clean of old leaves, blown-down twigs, anything they thought unsuitable or harmful for the tiny trout to live in. Marine biologists and chemists arrived to check for harmful bacteria. They also tested the pH and oxygen levels of the water, making sure it was suitable for a large number of trout.

On the special delivery day, many volunteers arrived. The trout pools were filled, dams were set in place, all made ready. Water quality was again checked by experts: was it cold enough? Pure enough? Bubbly enough to be a proper home for these baby fish?

The truck was too large to drive close, and the ground in the field too soft. Many volunteers were needed to make the transfer. Tiny fingerlings were gently netted from the truck's holding tank, slowly poured into clean white-plastic buckets. Volunteers formed a bucket brigade, each bucket carefully passed from one person to the next until it arrived at Pool #1 and Pool #2.

Beginning in August, Grandma and Grandpa — with

help from Fred, Max, Charles, their mother, and other special friends — would feed chow to the growing fish twice a day. It was a serious responsibility but one Grandpa particularly loved. He had a great respect for all trout but particularly his beloved brookies. From his own experience and from what he'd studied in books, Grandpa taught Max and Charles about brookies. They were known as the "noble, finicky, elitist trout." Unlike other fish and even unlike other trout, the brookie would thrive only in the purest water. Due to many forms of pollution, Grandpa and other serious fisherman and naturalists had sadly seen these fish decline over the years. In the world of trout, the wild brook trout is the fish that needs cold, natural spring water, well-aerated, an ideal pH, water no warmer than 55-65 degrees. Fish management experts came often to inspect and check for any fish illnesses or viruses.

Come spring, it was time to say goodbye to the trout. Again, many volunteers came and another truck and holding tank. This time the helpers used big nets, called seines: two-foot long bamboo poles with mesh tied between them. It was a two-person job, as the seines were lowered into the mass of swimming trout, then carefully lifted up.

Only clean, wet hands or hands wearing non-allergenic gloves could ever touch a fish. Gloved hands were used as trout were eased from seine into waiting buckets, filled with the same spring water they'd been nurtured in for the last nine months.

Someone had a record book to keep track of the number of brooks. Also recorded was their size: the length and weight of the fish of each type.

In good years, the brook trout had been 15-17 inches long, fat and healthy. The biggest, healthiest, small-hatchery fish raised in the area repeatedly came from Grandpa's. Max and Charles were proud of their grandpa and his friends and loved to see the certificates he earned for record-breaking numbers of big, healthy trout.

When all the fish were loaded, they were transported to streams where they would be protected as "Fish-for-Fun" trout. No one could catch them with barbed hooks. They were to be fished with barbless flies, and only fished by those who loved the challenge of fly-fishing. Some were even taken to Camp David, the U.S. President's official retreat in western Maryland, where many presidents spent quiet time fishing for Grandpa's trout.

Each summer, Grandpa kept a few trout as "pets." He and Grandma and other family members had to feed these lucky trout twice a day. Good weather or bad. In winter it could be icy, snowing, or raining, but the fish were fed. In late spring, Grandpa would pick four to six of the biggest, healthiest brookies and transport them to the Big Spring.

In the beginning, the pets were fed Trout Chow. Little by little they were weaned from bought food to the natural treats eaten by fish living in the wild. In their new habitat, this menu included nymphs under rocks, insects like May flies, minnows, other small fish, beetles, and ants that had slipped off rocks, twigs, blades of grass. And for the larger, feistier trout: crayfish.

Beside the Big Spring, Grandpa, Max and Charles sat still, listening to the burbling streams; breezes swishing through the long, yellow willow boughs; splashes as frogs leaped from grass into the cold water. Looking to the middle of the Big Spring, they could see three small springs stirring white sand and bits of black leaf and twigs as they bubbled up from the ground.

"You know," Grandpa said, "those springs are coming from deep, deep below. We're sitting on what's called an aquifer. Below us is an underground river, right here, right under us. Spring water is pure water, and a sign of pure water is watercress. It won't grow in polluted water. Where brookies thrive, we know the water is pure and drinkable. This is the water we drink. Each time you turn on the faucet in our house, you're turning on clean, safe spring water. Not only that, but it tastes good, too! And you know what?"

"What?" Charles asked as he scratched behind the ears of the now-quiet Fitz.

"Our water is the same as the Chattolanee Spring Water, which was so popular they bottled and sold it. But that was a long time ago."

"Wow," said Charles. He was thinking maybe he and Max should open a bottled water stand this summer. Sell Grandpa's spring water and not lemonade like most kids did. *'Spring Slam Water, Wash Away Your Thirst the Old-Fashioned Way. And It's Healthy, Too!'* Charles thought, inventing different sales pitches as he watched the spring's surface. Water skimmers (some called them water skaters) were sliding on the smooth surface. The water was so clear that deep down, on the sandy bottom, they could see the skimmers' shadows, legs like black lines, feet like little white bubbles.

It was very quiet in the spring. Too quiet. Something was not right.

"Look!" Max said. "I see two crayfish sparring, waving claws at each other, circling around near a carved-out smooth space."

"Max, an excellent find. That 'carved' place, as you said, is where a mama fish has made herself a nest. But where is she? Hmm, I don't see her, do you?"

Grandpa leaned forward. He pushed himself up until he was standing. His eyebrows narrowed and both boys could see he was concentrating on one spot. Looking carefully, Grandpa slowly stepped forward, peering into edgy places around the Big Spring. He stopped, stared in where a wily brook trout might be hiding in the shadows of long grassy overhangs, in notched, carved-away places, where once Native Americans dug clay for pots and other pottery.

"Boys, I don't like the looks of this. I'm afraid something bad has happened here. Something very, very bad; something scary, something sad."

"What?" Max and Charles said in unison.

Grandpa didn't answer. He was busy examining the Big Spring, the Little Spring, and the streams.

"It doesn't look good," was all he said. "It doesn't look good at all."

Chapter 3

My Pet Brookie is Missing!

Max had never seen Grandpa move so fast.

Imagine, Grandpa sprinting down the narrow path, springing over one of Fitz's dog toys, bouncing up the stone steps. He stopped there. His boots were muddy and he didn't want to track a mess over floors Grandma was mopping clean.

Behind him Fitz had run in long, looping circles, barking, yelping in her ear-ringing, high-pitched yips. Yappy heard Fitz and began baying as if following a rabbit trail.

Behind Fitz, Max and Charles jogged. Each carried a white bucket which bopped and banged against their skinny, naked legs.

'Some beautiful new bruises for sure,' Charles thought. *'By the time I see my friends in school on Monday, they'll be*

flowering purple. Badges of courage on my shins, earned by being there when Grandpa discovered his brookie was missing. Cool beans! Only it's very sad. And scary.'

"Robbed. Stolen. Who could have done such a mean thing?" Max muttered to himself.

"Who's so mean they'd take my Grandpa's pet brookie?"

"What in heaven's name is *this*?" Grandma asked in surprise. She opened the screen door with one hand, with the other she blocked their entrance into the glassed-in porch with the long, wooden handle of her big soggy floor mop.

"Our pet brookie has been stolen from the Big Spring," Grandpa said. He leaned his back against the shingled wall of the house and slid down until his bottom rested on the cement porch.

"Are you sure?"

"Looks that way. Later, alone, I'll creep up there with no dog or boys as company and see if maybe something spooked the pets today. But I don't think it looks good. Not good at all. Something stealing one or more of the biggest brookies means they might be coming in after sunset, with nets to dip, stealing some of the nearly grown trout in the pools." He turned to Max and Charles. "We forgot to put those screens back over #1 and #2. We'd best do it immediately or we'll make it too easy for something or somebody to come and fetch themselves some fish." He got up and stretched his back.

"Here, Grandma," Max said, handing her the white bucket filled with watercress. "Grandpa said you wanted some watercress today."

"And here, Grandma," Charles followed, holding out bunches of mint.

"Oh, you *are* good boys!" Grandma said. She put the mop to one side, closed the porch door and came out to where they were. She gave each a kiss on top of his head, including Grandpa. "Now you'd best get those screens in place, then sit down and plan what the next move should be."

They dragged the two heavy frames over the two trout pools.

And then:

Chapter 4

Chores to Do and 'No Way'

A Saturday at Grandma and Grandpa's meant fun, learning, and chores. Chores must always be done, no matter what drama might suddenly break into the routine, no matter what intruder might steal something valued by Grandma and Grandpa. Yes, the stolen fish was big news. It was something new for Grandma and Grandpa to discuss alone. After their discussion, Max and Charles might be included in a plan, but for now the plan was:

"Chores!" Grandma said. She came out onto the cement porch.

The boys were sitting on the top step with a pile of last year's acorns beside them. They were attempting to "sink" acorns between the roots of a large oak tree into a chipmunk hole. Perhaps the chipmunk had scurried deeper into its burrow or was just not home, because no furry creature came out to fuss at them.

"Saturday chores," said Grandma. "Max, will you please take these buckets into the meat house? I've taken the watercress out, thank you very much." She held up the buckets. "Now they need to be refilled halfway each. If you fill to the top, they're too heavy. Fill them from the big bags of chow. You know where they're stored?"

"In the old steel barrel with the wash tub lid and the cinder block on top?"

"Exactly. And don't forget to . . ."

"Replace the lid and the cinder block?"

"Smart boy. Bring back the white buckets. They go in the white-painted wardrobe here." She pointed to the wardrobe located in the corner of the glassed-in porch.

"Yes, ma'am."

"And Charles . . ."

'*Oh no,*' thought Charles, '*here it comes. I bet I know what my job will be.*'

"Yes, Grandma?"

"Charles, honey, I need you to clean up the yard. Definitely clean up around Yappy, but look for any 'surprises' Fitzgerald has left. Lately, she's left a few . . . unwanted gifts . . . under my clotheslines. I've learned the hard way to look before I step. It would be a kind act if someone would teach her better manners."

"OK, Grandma. Will do," said Charles. He couldn't help but wrinkle his nose.

"You know where to find the scooper and collection container?"

"Yep, back of the meat house."

"Thank you, Charles. It makes for one less chore I have to do," Grandma said, smiling.

"Afterwards?" Max asked.

"Afterwards, take the pony out and together you two can muck out her stall, give her clean straw bedding, hay, molasses feed, and a bucket of fresh water. If you'd like, take a ride or just exercise her on a lunge."

"Yes, ma'am!" Max and Charles said together. Taking care of the pony was less stinky and definitely more fun.

"By the time you get all those things done, I'm guessing it'll be close to 11:30. Charles, I see you have on your fancy wristwatch. And you both know what 11:30 means? Lunchtime. Keep one eye on your minutes. By lunch Grandpa and I might have an idea for the afternoon. Oh, and your Mom and Fred took baby Carrie with them to visit friends. They won't be back until late. I guess, unless you convince Ralph to babysi. . . I mean, keep you boys company, it might be best if you stay here tonight."

"Yes!"

"Great!"

Both boys were pleased. A night with their grandparents was never dull. Even though there were certain rules, like "no television, videos, or video games until after the 6 o'clock news," and then only if TV shows were educational, like a nature show, science, classical music concert, theatre performance, or a movie Grandma or Grandpa ranked A+. Otherwise, "television off." Grandpa often said, "TV is the biggest time-waster ever invented.

There are plenty of other things people should do with their time."

When staying with Grandma and Grandpa, Max and Charles knew there were many choices: chess and checker matches, Scrabble games, fly-tying, wood carving, carpentry lessons, art supplies, books of all kinds for all ages stacked everywhere, many unusual musical instruments from different countries to experiment with, animal training, walks, learning about gardening and tree-keeping, canning, cooking, and hunting for arrowheads.

The Property, as Grandma and Grandpa's farm was called long ago, had been the camp of Native Americans. Some things they left had been found in many areas of the Property, in streams, the Grove, and Grandpa's garden: arrowheads, bird points, spears, scrapers, and soapstone pottery. Whenever it rained or when Grandpa ran the rototiller in the garden, planted seeds, picked fruits and vegetables, or even pulled weeds, he found more treasures. People said Grandpa had an eye for spotting artifacts. Over many years he'd gathered a collection which filled boxes and boxes. He'd lived on the Property ever since he was seven; Max and Charles' mom was raised there, and now Max and Charles lived there, though not in the original house. But of all who lived or visited this small farm, no one could spot an arrowhead like Grandpa.

With all these activities for Max and Charles, including looking at the collection of artifacts and trying to find their own, the "no TV" rule was no big deal.

Max and Charles finished all the dirty work. Now it was time to take care of NoWay, the Welsh pony.

NoWay was a barrel-bellied pinto, gentle but stubborn. Her favorite gait choice was not a gallop, rocking horse canter, or bouncy up/down trot. What NoWay preferred was to walk. Not even a steady-paced walk. A walk for NoWay was start, stop, graze, "OK." Start, "hmm," stop, graze.

She was a beginner rider's perfect pony. She would never bite, bulk, buck, or rear up. She would never roll or rub someone against a building when they tried to ride her.

Grandma, who bought her for the boys, had ridden steeplechase and woodland trails from the time she was a child until after she married Grandpa. Grandpa had also ridden as a child, and now he treated NoWay, the other ponies, and horses the way he treated dogs. He scratched them behind their ears, enjoyed "horsing" around with them, but would never ride.

On this May 1 Saturday, Max stepped onto the designated "climbing up" log next to the pony shed. He popped onto NoWay's back. Charles followed Max, who gave him a pull up. Both boys took a short ride on NoWay down to the farm pond and back to her stall.

Charles checked his watch. "11:00," he announced.

"That means we have 30 minutes before lunch, said Max. "What do you suggest we do?"

Chapter 5

Northern Red Salamanders on a Free Ride and Clean-Up Time

"Ah, hmm. Oh . . . Hey, want to check for salamanders and get a drink of icy water from the other spring?"

"Sure."

"Race you." Charles took off across the side yard to what the family called the Grove. He was a fast sprinter and beat Max by two seconds.

"You should be competing at school. You're really fast for an eight-year-old," Max said, panting.

"Oh, you slowed so I could beat you."

"No way! I was in fifth gear. You're really fast. But then you're skinny and all muscle," Max said, looking at his younger brother.

It was true. Charles, though he was someone with his head in math or science almost 24/7, loved spending hours on woods trails with Grandpa or Fred. All year,

Charles was on a swim team and he'd won enough ribbons and trophies to almost fill a room.

Max loved to swim, too, but he was lazy swimmer. Grandpa had taught him the side stroke, breast stroke, back stroke, and how to float. Max excelled at floating. In fact, his favorite swim times were riding on ocean waves or resting back on pond and lake waters. He'd swim out beyond the sandy beach, where toddlers played, or away from rocks where cannonball dives were the way middle teens (fourteen to seventeen) liked to entertain their would-be dates. Max went where the water was calm. When he was alone, he'd float on his back, watching clouds skim across blue skies. On late summer and early fall days, neon blue or green dragon flies hovered in the air near his wiggling toes. He was not one to compete in sports, preferring to zone out and be "in the moment."

Together the boys went to the covered spring. A concrete tube two feet in diameter by four feet long had been sunk vertically into the spongy ground to form a protective wall around the spring. On top was an aging, warped plywood board held in place by a cinder block (Grandpa's favorite choice for weighing objects down). A few feet from the spring was a forked stick, and hanging from it a small tin cup. On hot humid summer days, this spring was a favorite spot for icy cold drinks of water.

But first: where were the salamanders?

The boys crept close to the spring. Three feet to go before the spring. They went down onto their knees until they were eye level with the edges of the plywood. They slowly inched across the mossy moist ground. Not a word, not a whisper. They hardly dared to breathe as they advanced into the world of the slimy, skittery, slithery northern red salamanders.

Max made eye contact with Charles, signaling: There they are.

And there they were. Two, three, four, six salamanders, some next to the plywood, others on it, two more hung on the side of the cement tube looking like Christmas trim on a bookshelf or fireplace mantle. All were red with black spots; some were small, but one was almost seven inches long.

"Six?" Charles mouthed.

Max nodded.

Now what?

Should they try their luck at nabbing one without hurting it, or be wildlife observers and watch what salamanders do?

Max and Charles opted to watch, not snatch. But there was a catch: in order to get a cool drink from the spring, they had to remove the plywood and cinder block.

Max whispered, "Let's try and slide it open wide enough to get a drink."

"OK," Charles whispered back.

The boys crawled backwards until they were about three feet away. Slowly they stood. Both rubbed knees, which now were the color of rich back mud. Max slipped the cup from the stick so they'd have it. "OK," he said "the plan is . . ."

"Yes?"

"Well, I'm thinking," said Max.

"Why not do what we've done before . . . the old tried and true."

"And that was?"

"We both go around to the back, behind those bushes, and we 'one, two, three, push' the board far enough so we can get a drink of water."

"Not a hard push because if we did, we'd be 'rubbing out' salamanders and sending them to salamander heaven, or wherever salamanders go."

"A slow, steady push-ush-ush-push. Maybe, if we push slow enough, it'll be like nudging salamanders along, you know, the way a big stone is pushed when someone grades a new road or in winter when a big frozen block of icy snow is pushed out to sea," said Charles.

"Well, we'll try," said Max.

Time for "stealth-stepping" the way Grandpa had taught them. Don't break the smallest twig or crunch a dried crisp leaf, but instead, ease toes underneath everything that might make a noise. It was hard but not impossible. It required moving slow and being aware.

Next, they had to bend under the hemlock bush that shaded the spring. The boys, each using both hands, began an inch-by-inch push. They took their time as Grandpa often instructed: "Always take your time, never rush or move too quickly or you might lose it all."

An inch, another, then another. Slowly and carefully they moved the board, and as they did, they stole glances and winked at each other. A couple of shade-basking salamanders were not aware they were getting a free ride.

Max stopped the push me/slide me when half of the

protected spring was uncovered. "Now, let's enjoy some of the best spring water around," he said softly.

Again both boys got on hands and knees and crawled to where the open spring and icy water waited. And wonder of wonder, even after such a ride, several salamanders were still on the wood, seeming to be quite content to stay there.

Dip, drink, share. Dip, drink, share. And as they drank, Max and Charles watched two more salamanders scramble over tiny quartz stones and scurry up the sides of the cement tube. Looking down, down, four feet to the bottom of the spring, they watched the churning of white sand and black leaves moving up from deep below. And, as they watched, two more salamanders slid to a wet shelter between the cement pipe and the stream bank.

Moments later, one last official count, then Max and Charles were sliding the board back with ten salamanders enjoying a free ride.

"OK, we need to quickly get rid of some of this muck and be on time for 11:30 lunch," Charles warned.

They set all in order in two minutes, including replacing the tin cup on the forked stick. They ran barefooted across soft green moss that grew nowhere else on the Property in the same way as it did in the Grove.

From the time they were able to listen, Grandpa had told them about the moss and the mound of round gray stones in the Grove. Some people thought, including Grandpa, that these stones were part of an ancient burial ground. Each of the stones was the same size and each fit in the palm of Grandpa's hand. Under these stones, the soil was different: black-gray, ash-like, powdery. When you were in this place of bright green moss and round gray stones, there was this strange and knowing type of feeling that the Grove was a special place and had been special for centuries.

Time check: "We have enough time for a one-minute ride each on the Tree Horse," Charles told Max.

"Then let's do it! One never knows what the wind might do to our favorite tree."

"Or some stupid robber who might also take trees," Charles said darkly.

The Tree Horse was a white birch tree their mother had shown Max when he was about three or four years old.

'This was my Tree Horse. I found it when I was a little girl, Max,' Mom had said. *'You slide on the saddle part, put both hands on the trunk, and hold onto what looks like a neck that stretches upward. You shake the trunk neck and bounce on the saddle part, and if feels as if you are trotting. When you do, if you do it just right, the entire tree will trot, too, and you'll feel like you're riding a horse into the sky!'*

Whenever Max and Charles had time alone in the Grove, they always climbed aboard the Tree Horse, and always, so far, had special rides. It was the same on this Saturday. The white birch trotted, and way up on the "neck," tiny spring leaves fluttered.

"Now, we really have to 'make tracks', as Grandpa always says," said Charles, looking at his watch. "Time is ticking away."

Both boys raced back to the cement porch. They

arrived at 11:24. They washed the worst of the muck off with the outside hose and dried their legs, arms, and hands with a few old dish towels Grandma left for them on the porch.

11:26 — They knocked on the back door.

11:27 — Grandma came out to inspect them.

"Not bad, considering the muck you've been in. Now, beeline upstairs, use some soap. Here. *Here*! Use paper towels." She handed each boy two folded, extra-thick paper towels. "I want to save the fancy cloth towel with the 'high thread count' decorated with cross-stitched country scenes. Those are special towels for visitors from away who are over twenty years old."

"OK, Grandma. We will, Grandma!" Max and Charles dashed through the darkened dining room (it was used only for special events), up the steep steps and down the hall to the bathroom.

"Lifebuoy or the tried-and-true Ivory?" Max asked, holding up two bars of soap.

Charles grabbed the Lifebuoy. Max chose Ivory, the soap he knew Grandpa always used.

At exactly 11:30 the boys entered the kitchen smelling sweet and looking almost clean. True, they had missed a few places. Slashes of black mud still marked legs and arms. Charles wore two spots on his face, which looked like theatre paint, one on each side of his nose dipping to the middle of his cheeks. But after the busy morning they'd had and after where they'd been, they looked clean enough.

"Have a seat!" commanded Grandpa.

They took the same seats they'd used for breakfast.

Grandma brought to the table two platters of sandwiches of all kinds: ham and cheese, egg salad, peanut butter with her famous strawberry jam from last spring's strawberries, and, of course, watercress and homemade butter on white bread with crusts cut off. Next came two icy cold metal pitchers:

"This one, with ALT initials, is sweet tea. The one with SJY is tangy lemonade sweetened with real maple sugar. And here," she said, turning and picking up a tiny cutting board and placing it in the center of the table, "here is some of the mint you picked. Now it's ready for whichever drink you pick."

"A feast!" Grandpa declared. "Eat. Chew slowly and quietly. Your grandma and I have a plan."

Chapter 6

The Plan is Revealed

Max and Charles chewed slowly with mouths closed and ears open, listening as Grandpa unveiled The Plan and Grandma added details.

"How brave are you two boys? No, don't answer me. I know. Your Grandma and I have a plan. It calls for two brave boys, but we don't believe it's dangerous."

"We don't want you to be in danger," Grandma said.

"Scary is not always dangerous. Scary can be when our imaginations make us feel like something is worse than it really is, when something is going to hurt us when it really isn't. You can be near a scary situation, but that doesn't mean you have to experience it. Is that clear as mud?" Grandpa asked.

Charles nodded.

Max gulped down his small bite of sandwich and said,

"Yes."

"I know you both are wondering what I just said. Because it is confusing, so let me tell you a story as an example," Grandpa said.

"OK," Max said.

Charles chewed and nodded in agreement.

"Once, when I was somewhere between the two of you in age, I was out in the middle of woods here on the Property, and a mighty storm came up. It was wind like a giant snoring. It was thunder like the booms made when Douglas fir trees fall . . . those are the big ones on the West Coast. People drive cars through Douglas firs. You know, I've shown you pictures."

Both boys nodded.

"Trees big as this kitchen," Grandma added.

"Just about," Grandpa agreed.

"Wow," said Charles. He swallowed and reached for his lemonade.

"It began to rain. Some say it can rain 'buckets.' On this day, it didn't rain buckets, it rained mighty waterfalls. It rained Niagara Falls, like the Horseshoe Falls on Canada's side. And I was a long way from home."

"I started running from one hairy monster evergreen to the next, because their boughs can keep off some of the wet. But I was soaked. Then I heard something very scary. Way in the distance I heard it. Like a big old freight train barreling down a track, I heard it. And it was coming . . ." He stopped to take another bite of his ham and cheese sandwich. He took a long drink of sweet tea. He let what he had said sink in.

"Thunder," whispered Charles.

"And lightning?" added Max in a small voice.

"You're right," said Grandpa. "I heard thunder. It was in the distance, but with each rumbling I knew it was getting closer. And thunder and lightning and trees . . . now that's not a good combination. But I knew where I was in the woods. I was in the part where the limestone cutters used to live in simple houses. And I knew there was one not too far away. If I could only run there fast enough."

"You are a fast runner, Grandpa," Charles said.

"We saw you run today, so we know," Max added.

"I was. I was a runner. I competed in cross-country way back when I was young," Grandpa smiled, then continued. "I began to run. I was running faster than I'd ever had to run in any race I had ever run. And soon I saw it. I saw the old Limestone Cutter's house. And I ran for it."

"Good!" Charles said.

"Excellent," added Max.

"Nope," said Grandpa. "It was Old Jim's house. Old Jim was meaner than a copperhead. To make bad go to worse, he'd been to my father complaining about my behavior . . . but that's a story for another day and time." Grandpa took another bite, chewed, and drank another long swig of mint-flavored tea.

Meanwhile, Max and Charles looked at each other. They knew Grandma called Grandpa a rascal, as did their mother, they just didn't know exactly what that meant.

"I'll write a note and put it on our refrigerator to

remind Grandpa to tell you two more stories about Jim," Grandma said with a grin.

"I heard the thunder. It was closer. The wind was blowing so hard, treetops were making bigger and bigger circles around and around. Some neighbor trees, which had stood side by side all of their long lives, not touching, now they were bumping heavy high trunks against each other: 'Boom! Boom! Boom!' It was nice they were getting to know each other better, but I was hoping, yep, even praying, they'd not get in a fight and try to knock each other so hard one would fall over."

He looked at the boys to make sure they were listening and was met with wide eyes, mouths no longer chewing, not reaching for something more to drink. Now, the boys were really listening. Grandpa liked to have people listening and hanging on to every word and every pause between words when he told a story.

"There came then a huge crash. It sounded like it was less than a hundred feet from where I was. Well, it scared me so bad I was no longer worrying about Jim and what he might be thinking of me. I knew I had to get in his house and get in there fast. I ran the final distance, knocked on Jim's door yelling, *'For the love of everything, Jim, it's me, please let me in!'* "

Grandpa took another long drink. He wanted his words to settle into the boys' minds and hearts. This was an important part of the story.

"The door opened. It opened immediately. There was Jim in red long johns, a pair of dirty bibbed overalls, and that was about it. *'For the love of . . . Boy, get your hide in here before you get us both kilt!'* Jim said. He grabbed me by my soaking wet shirt collar and yanked me into his smoky, lamp-lit cabin just as another 'BAM' of thunder came. The cabin door was shut when we heard and saw what happened next. We could see it through a small, four-paned window: this giant bolt of lightning came searing down the side of a tremendous cedar tree . . . about a foot from where seconds ago I'd been standing. The lightning kept hitting the tree. It was like: 'BAM! BLAM! BLAMMMM.' Fire shooting out. Needles and bark sizzling. Then . . . all we heard was rain, rain, waterfall rain washing over everything. The rain was a blessing. Oh yes, indeed it was! It kept away a mighty fire from burning all the woods, Jim and me, and I don't know what all, with it."

"Wow."

"Scary," whispered Max.

"There we were, Jim and me. Lifelong enemies saved by something . . . standing beside each other in Jim's little old shack. And Jim smelled like he hadn't had a bath for months. He was about the rankest smelling person I'd ever met. But more, there was also this tangy sweet fragrance which comes from someone's mouth, someone who's been enjoying his old brown jug filled with illegal, homemade, what they used to call moonshine."

"I won't lie to you, boys. I was scared. And old Jim said to me, *'Here boy, take a swig of this. It'll warm you from your insides out to your thin skin and those hairs that are sticking straight up. It'll calm what's making you shake like a rattlesnake's tail when he's scared and wants to warn off danger'.* " "To be honest, Charles and Max, I did take the jug from Jim. I did take a gulp. I never ever did drink anything quite like it. And I hope to never ever drink anything like it again. It was fire ... like the lightning fire that had whammed the cedar tree. My insides burned from my lips to my tongue to my throat all the way down to where there was no place else to go and still I was burning. I also felt suddenly very tired."

"Jim knew. He pulled a chair up and made me sit by his smoky fire. I sat and felt the warm inside of me and, by that old woodstove, my outsides were warming, too. And in my head, I felt the thunder, the lightning, and the great winds getting smaller and smaller. I don't think I passed out, but I have to admit, things were awfully quiet all around me, blurry, sort of comfy, too."

"Rain kept falling and I was glad to be inside away from it. Jim, he treated me like an important guest, not like an archenemy. He was a gentleman . . . Oh, he was rough, and he did stink, but he was a gentleman all the same. He thought I might be hungry and he wanted to feed me up good. Warming in a pan with a cloth over it was something that smelled like something good my mom would have baked. Jim went over and pulled off the cloth. I saw it was a loaf of some sort of bread. From a big hook hung on the wall, Jim took a carving knife. He cut two big hunks out of the loaf, and he put each on a tin plate. He wiped the knife on the cloth, covered the loaf, and brought the plates over."

" 'Here, made this corn bread earlier today. My mamma taught me you never let company come and not have something nourishing to offer them. It's important to have hospitality.' "

" '*Thank you, Jim. Thank you, I'm feeling empty inside,*' " I said. I bit into warm cornbread. I'd never tasted something so good and I don't know if I ever have again . . . not to say your grandma isn't one of the greatest cooks . . . something a rascal like me never deserved." Grandpa gave Grandma a big smile.

"And it looks like now I have to dig around in my cookbooks and find a recipe for cornbread that might taste half as special as what Jim gave you. I'll bake it up for supper tonight, I will," said Grandma.

"Oh now, boys, I think Grandma is going to spoil us mighty good."

"Grandpa, what happened next?" Charles said.

"Oh, my . . . and now it's time for the rest of the story," Grandpa said with a grin. "I ate the cornbread and Jim offered me more from his little brown jug, but I declined. He had some spring water in a big gallon jar and a tin cup like the one we keep by the spring. Jim's water tasted real fine. By the time I'd eaten the hunk of cornbread, the storm had passed and the rain had eased up until it wasn't more than a sprinkle. I wasn't totally dry, but I wasn't soaked anymore and I was warmed up good inside and out. I stood up and the room didn't spin so I knew I could walk. '*Jim,*' I said, '*I think Ma might be worried something might have happened to me awfully bad. I'd best be making my way home.*'

And he agreed. '*A son shouldn't be bringin' worry to his mum. I think the storm has passed, but just in case, boy, you run straight home as fast as you can run,*' Jim said.

"And you did," Grandma said. "But that's not the end

of the story. Even though your Grandpa and Jim had never been friends before, the storm changed things. Grandpa began visiting Jim and taking him good things like slabs of bacon and baked cookies his mother had made."

"This is true," said Grandpa. "And in the little bit of time I knew Jim after that stormy day, I learned all about him and why he was the way he was and more. I learned about how it's no good to make a judgment without knowing all the facts. No pointing fingers at someone and judging, that's just not right." He paused and drank some more sweet tea. "Yeah, it was a scary day. And yep, I was one scared pup having to ask for help from someone I'd been mean to. But I learned. So, you see, scary can be good . . . and it can also be bad. It's bad when it keeps us from learning."

"Now for the plan," Grandma said. "Grandpa and I think if you two boys pitch a tent partway between the Big Spring and the house and spend the night there, we might learn who's stealing our favorite brook trout." She put some homemade strawberry pie down on the table.

"Ah, but I'm not sure where Fred has packed our tents," Max said. He was not sure he could eat any pie. His scary feeling was beginning.

"Oh, your tent isn't needed," Grandpa said. "We have a good canvas tent."

"Our sleeping bags . . . I'm not sure where Fred and Mom have stored them," Charles said. His scary was also beginning, strong as the big storm from Grandpa's story.

"No need for sleeping bags. I know of something much

better. In the trunks we have many of Great-Grandma's down comforters. Two of those on the floor of the tent, with a queen-size sheet and summer-weight blanket, and you two will be comfy as can be."

"Ah, OK. But you think we'll be safe?" Max asked.

"Well, I'm no gambler. I pledged when I was a child never to gamble and I never have, if you take out the exception of marrying Grandpa. Now, come to think of it, that was a risky, gambling like action, but it all worked out OK." Grandma rubbed the top of Grandpa's crew-cut head. He smiled.

"Watch it, Grandma, boys this age don't like 'mushy stuff', " he said. "And if you really feel you need protection, there's Fitzgerald here to keep you company."

"Ah, OK. I mean if you're sure," said Max, thinking to himself, *'I mean if a boy can't trust his grandparents, then who can he trust?'*

"And you, Charles?"

"Count me in," Charles said. *'Someone has to be there to look after Max,'* he thought.

"Wunnerful, wunnerful," Grandma said in her best Lawrence Welk imitation. "Soon as you finish your dessert, you'd best go get the tent and comforters. They'll need some airing. While you get them, I'll take the dry clothes off the lines. By dinner time they should be aired out."

"The tent we'll set up. It will be the best way for it to air. It's heavy canvas, not like your little pop-ups. This tent was made to last for years and it has," said Grandpa.

"So, we have a plan," Grandma said. She started cutting

a double-size piece of pie for all "the men" and a single slice for herself. She watched her weight, or, as she often said, "my girlish figure."

The pie was warm and yummy. One of Max and Charles' favorites. All was eaten and their plates licked clean, although, in fact, they scraped the dessert plates with their forks, not tongues.

"OK. Back to the project. You boys go get comforters and tent while I get the clothes," said Grandma.

"And I'll go to the shed and get the hammer and some extra ropes for the tent," said Grandpa.

"And we'll go . . . ah, Grandma, Grandpa, where will Charles and I go to get the comforters and tent?" Max asked.

"Why, I'm sorry, thought you knew. Up in the attic. When you get up there, look on the right. First trunk you see will have lots of comforters. Stay on the right, but go back under the eaves and you'll find a canvas knapsack containing the tent," said Grandma. She took two flashlights and handed them to the boys. Then she opened a spare coffee canister and took out two packages of batteries. "Just in case one flashlight burns out, here are some extra batteries. But there's a ceiling bulb and big windows at each end of the attic. On a bright day like today, you should see just fine."

"Remember, there's no floor. So don't step off the path of old doors when you're up there, or off the beams. Especially, don't step down into that fuzzy, wooly stuff because even though you two are under 100 pounds, you may break through and come crashing through the ceiling. I'm sure that's not what you want to do. It would be a big mess to clean up and the old-fashioned wallpaper may be hard to replace," said Grandpa calmly.

"OoooooooOK," Max said. His heart was beating "boom-boom-boom" already.

"OK," said Charles, as his heart also went "boom, boom, boom."

Chapter 7

No! Not the Attic! Anything but the Attic!

Grandma and Grandpa were both outside. Grandma was carrying in laundry. Grandpa was collecting things he needed to set up the tent.

Charles looked at Max.

Max looked at Charles.

Charles finally asked, "I mean, why is it everything we need is in the attic?"

Max nodded.

Charles continued, "I mean, we made a pact after the last time we went up there. I remember exactly what we said: 'No! No! Not the Attic!' We'd go anywhere and do everything for Grandma and Grandpa, but 'anything but the attic!' "

"I know. But hey, we have flashlights and we have each other. Grandpa told us a great story about feeling scared. We didn't have power before when we went up into the attic. This time we are powered up with an important mission!" Max said.

"So, let's do it! Before our powered-up begins powering down."

The two boys headed for the stairs. They climbed the steep flight to the second floor. They went down the long, darkened hallway and opened the door to the furnished bedroom no one slept in anymore. It smelled faintly like ladies' perfume and powders. It had been Great-Grandmother's room. Their aunt had asked Grandma and Grandpa to always leave it the way it was when she died: clean, straight, everything in the same place where it had been. It was a museum. The boys quickly looked around, then headed deeper into the room to a dark corner where the attic door was located.

Turning the knob, they discovered it was locked. But they knew where the key was . . . under a dusty seashell on top of a chest of drawers across from the attic door. Great-Grandmother had kept it there.

Max got the key.

For a moment the boys stood together in the Museum.

"She was a nice lady, or so everyone says," Max said.

"Look at all the pictures of angels . . . in every picture angels are looking . . . at us. That's a good thing, right? Angels don't hang around in bad places," Charles said.

"This room is the easy part. The attic is the challenge. Are you ready, little bro?" Max asked. "Flashlights on."

Both boys switched black buttons into the "on" position. The Museum was now filled with two spot-like bright lights.

"Ready, set . . ." Max turned the key and the lock clicked opened.

"One. Two. Three. Here we go!"

Max pulled the door open. The boys looked up into the eerie, dark attic.

"Don't forget the pull chain," reminded Charles.

"Yeah, thanks." Max looked for the almost invisible fishing line. He found it: lower left under the stair rail. He remembered to pull the line down. When he did, a single 60-watt bulb at the top of the stairs came on. One bulb, and sunlight struggling through the dusty windows at both ends of the long, dark attic, an attic filled wall-to-ceiling with lifetimes of "stuff." One bulb, dim sunlight, and now two flashlights added up to the only light in that dark cavern.

"Well, I pulled the string to light our path. Now, I think you should be the one who walks up the stairs first," Max said.

"What? No, really?"

"Look at it this way. I'll have your back covered."

"OK, OK, but you know what? If I turn suddenly and begin making a quick exit and you're there behind me .. . I'll knock into you on my way down. It'll be just like Jack and Jill, and you're Jack who breaks his crown."

"Yeah, smarty, and so who does that make you? 'And Jill came tumbling after.'" Max knew his nursery rhymes.

"I'm no Jill! OK, OK. I'll make the first step up, but you know what? Jack breaks his crown and others in the rhyme only tumble. OK, here I go. Watch me as I go. I'm going now. I'm lifting up my leg. I'm putting my foot down on step #1," Charles said in slow motion. He switched on his flashlight and started up the attic stairs.

Each step was a step into the past, and deep, dark, dusty old seemed to close around him and with it the odor of mothballs.

Max watched Charles. When Charles had gotten as far as step #5, Max guiltily followed his younger brother.

At the top of the stairs, both boys stood side by side. They slowly turned clockwise, attempting to see as much of the attic as they could see, at the same time looking for quick getaway routes.

The attic was another world, a place where memories of past ways and past lives were stored. It was here where old wardrobes had been moved, and inside of them? There were schooner trunks from when members of the family arrived from Ireland (before the potato blight), Germany (in the 1850s), Russia (in 1910), trunks packed and sent home from World War II war zones, or several that Grandma brought with her when she married Grandpa.

Along one side of the long, open space were rods paralleling the ceiling. Hanging from these rods, inside of plastic and durable red-brown paper, were clothes: fancy clothes once worn by members of the family who now had been dead a hundred years or more. Hung with the clothes were boots, shoes, ropes, life jackets.

Everywhere in the attic were boxes: some stacked to the ceiling, others, like the ones Grandma stored "Christmas" in, were within easy reach.

Back in the dark under the eaves were pictures of

people: couples dressed in wedding clothes, children looking disgruntled, old houses, horses, formal gardens with roses blooming, landscapes showing flocks of sheep peacefully roaming over fields of grass, and sepia-tinted, fat cherubs grinning, looking "right into your eyes," Charles said.

Tangled arms and legs of chairs and tables were stacked in dark places or hung from hooks. Those facing the stairs seemed to beg visitors, "Please sit, it has been years since anyone needed me." All silently seemed to be staring at visitors, daring them to come closer, closer, perhaps daring them to make a change.

Near the window which looked out onto the Grove was the rocking horse Max and Charles had rocked on and which would certainly be taken down, washed, and used for their baby sister Carrie when she was big enough. In that same section were other toys: a doll house Grandpa had made Mom and a toy bassinette that Mom had rocked baby puppies in, not dolls.

One could have explored the attic for days and not seen everything stored there. It would seem like the perfect place for boys to make discoveries. But there was this spooky sense of strange silence: a place filled with wrapped-up, locked-away, stored hopes, dreams, and this haunting feeling that at any moment something unreal, unnatural, supernatural might happen.

"Grandpa said the tent was . . .?" Charles asked.

"Top of stairs on right, under the eaves, in a big duffle bag," Max rattled off in a trembling voice. He had the creeps, but he wasn't going to tell his little brother.

Instead, he shone his flashlight where he thought the tent might be. "Yes!" There was a long, tan, body-bag shaped thing with a leather strap. "That must be it. See if you can get to it. Remember to walk on the doors or on the rafters, because they are the floor up here, but don't . . ."

"I know, 'Don't step into the white stuff that looks like sheep wool because under it is the ceiling and it isn't strong and one could break through.'"

"Right."

"Why me? Why me alone? Come over here, Max. It looks like it might be heavy," Charles said. He carefully stepped deeper into the eave space where the duffle bag was stored.

Max felt guilty. He moved to help Charles. He kept the light on the spot where Charles was and to where he was headed.

"Yeah, this is it," Charles said. "Whoa! It's heavy. I think we both need to get it and we're going to need all four hands . . ."

"Which means we need to put our flashlights down and keep them shining where we need to see. We need to wedge them in places where they won't roll away, fall, snap out, or break."

"Right," Charles said. He shone his flashlight around the attic. "Aha!" Above his head a cane chair hung on a hook. Charles wedged the flashlight into the mesh of broken cane. "Look, Max, perfect."

"Don't brag, Charles, be humble. I think we don't want to upset any . . . We don't want to change anything. Be respectful in this place, 'cause we're just a couple of kids."

"OK."

Max beamed his light around for a place to safely lodge it. At last he saw where he could put it, where it wouldn't fall or roll, where it would hopefully be useful . . . a rope hanging over one of the clothes rods. Perfect. Max took hold of it. It was tied around the pole with one long end free. Max made a slipknot the way Grandpa had taught him and tied the flashlight in place. When he let go, it rocked like a pendulum back and forth, back and forth until finally it was motionless. *'In a way, it's scarier motionless than when it's rocking,'* Max thought.

Max tiptoed across two white doors. They squeaked, giving in a little under his weight. *'That's reassuring. Not,'* he thought. He stepped onto a three-inch-wide ceiling joist and reached up to the roof braces, holding one to help balance himself. He was next to Charles.

"See, Max, this is the duffle bag. This has got to be it. Look, there's a label." He reached down, turned it over, and showed a leather holder with a yellowed plastic protector. With the dim light and the faded ink, the boys could just make out Grandpa's name and the address of the Property, minus a road number and zip code.

"Yep. Confirmed. Good job, Charles," Max said. "Can you push it over closer? I'll pull it."

"OK." Charles sat down on the floor joists and began pushing the duffle bag until he had dislodged it from where it had nestled. He pushed and finally got it loose, then slid it across an unpainted wooden door and closer to Max.

Still with a tight grip on a roof beam, Max bent down

and began pulling the bag, with Charles pushing from behind. Working together, the boys were able to get it to the top of the stairs. "Now all we have to do is give it a push and it will roll down by its self," Max said, glad to be on solid footing once more. He started untying the flashlight from the rope, while Charles walked "the balance beam" back to the chair and pulled his flashlight free from the rope.

Charles was soon back beside Max, standing on the wide, safe door. They were ready for the next step: finding the comforters.

"Where did Grandma say they were again?" Charles asked.

"In a trunk," Max said.

"Oh, great, there are about a hundred trunks!"

"Yeah, I know, but she said it was close to where we're standing now."

"Well, there's this one," Charles said. He moved to a black trunk with a rounded top.

"Or this one," said Max, stepping to another. It was also round-topped, wedged in a space between wardrobes. Above it, one of the clothes rods was attached to a ceiling beam. On the end of the rod, the very end and closest to Max, a pair of fishing waders hung down. *'Must be Grandpa's other pair,'* Max thought. But the creepy feeling went over him again. He wished his imagination wasn't so active. *'Or a pair for a ghost to step into and go walking again.'* He dared not say his thoughts out loud, no sense in freaking out Charles.

"Let's open both and see if one of them has the comforters," Charles said.

'*Man, he sure is acting brave. Wish I was as brave,*' thought Max.

'*Wow, Max is braver than I ever knew,*' thought Charles.

Max went to the schooner trunk closest to him. It had a metal lock with a keyhole in front. '*I wonder if I need a key.*' He pushed the shackle up and out of the way, then began raising the lid. It lifted easily. Inside, he saw several shirt boxes, and under them a pair of men's leather riding boots. Then came a bigger box, the size a jacket might come in. Max kept lifting things out and piling them carefully on the door-floor. Then a small ring box, but when he opened it, the place where the ring would be was empty. '*Looks like the guy who owned this trunk gave some lady a ring,*' Max thought. Under all the boxes was a thick, greenish-brown wool blanket like those issued to soldiers. And under it . . .

"WOW!"

"What?" Charles said, looking up.

"A belt, a holster and inside of it . . . I think . . ." With both hands, Max lifted up the belt with holster attached. It was heavier than just leather. He put it on the door and sat down beside it.

Charles couldn't stand the suspense any longer. He returned to Max's side. "Do you think . . ."

"There's only way to find out." Max took both his thumbs and pushed them under the flap, beside a brass snap. He pushed as hard as he could and the snap let go. The leather flap didn't move. It had stayed in the same position for many years. Max lifted the stiff leather and there it was: a pistol.

"Are you going to remove it?" Charles asked.

"No, but I am going to tell Grandma and Grandpa about it. They should know," said Max. He didn't try to snap the snap back. He didn't think it really mattered. He returned the belt and holster to the trunk.

"But who do you think owns it . . . owned it?"

"I'm not sure, but maybe one of these other boxes will help us know more."

And they did.

Inside the biggest box was a World War II Army general's brown dress jacket. No names but plenty of stripes and buttons. Inside smaller dress shirt boxes were . . . dress shirts, some Army issue, others for more formal occasions. Each shirt was carefully wrapped in white tissue and looked as if it had just arrived: spotlessly clean, starched collars, ironed, packaged, and sent to the owner from a commercial cleaner. In one little box, they saw a medal. Max recognized it: "A Purple Heart." In other boxes were cuff links, a high school ring engraved with '1941' and the school name. Not one Max or Charles recognized.

Another box contained several books. Max opened one, saw it was a journal, and immediately closed it. He didn't think an eleven-year-old boy should be reading a soldier's personal journal. Another box was filled with letters and three photos: one was a beautiful woman, one a handsome man in Army dress uniform, and one of the two of them together, the woman holding a baby boy.

"Who are these people?" Charles asked.

"I think it might be Grandpa's sister, her husband, and

their son. I know our Mom's uncle was in World War II. They don't live near here. Not sure why their stuff is here." Max put everything back as he had found it, as best as he could. He closed the trunk lid. "Maybe when we tell Grandpa and Grandma about the pistol, they'll decide what to do with it. And tell us why it's here."

"Or not," said Charles.

"Or not. OK, time to check what's in your trunk."

Charles crawled over many obstacles: a pile of summer rugs for every room in the house, lumpy cloth bags with maybe more clothes in them, boxes marked "games and puzzles," tied up with twine. Finally, he arrived back to the trunk he'd chosen to open.

"Is it locked?"

"Nope."

"Can you lift it open?"

"Maybe." Charles pulled the metal flap away from the steel latch. With both hands he pushed on the lid with all his strength. The lid moved, creaking, then bounced open, as if it were on a spring.

"Ahhhhhhhh-ohhhhhhhhhhh. Yuck!" Charles screamed.

He backed up until he was dangerously close to stepping into the fuzzy insulation.

Max was ready to run down the steps and get out of the attic to safety, as quick as possible, every boy for himself, but something stopped him. Charles was not running away, even though he had screamed and almost stepped through the ceiling. He was still looking in the trunk.

"What!!! What is it?"

Charles dropped his head between his knees trying to

catch his breath. When he stood straight again, his face was red. His lips were tipping into a smile. "Whew! I didn't expect this! Hah! Someone was really pulling a joke. I wonder if it was Grandpa?"

"Hurry and tell me!" Max said.

"Tell you? Hah! I'll show you." Charles stepped back to the trunk. He reached in and seconds later he had pulled out a head.

"Ahhhhhhhhhhhh! Whattttt?" Max screamed.

"Ha! Scared you, too! It scared an eleven-year-old as badly as it did little ol' me, an eight-year-old."

Charles was holding, by a cloth loop in the top of its head, a human head-size coconut with carved face. It had white shell ears hanging from frayed pink cloth on each side, two large white shell eyes with black pupils, and in the blood-red, carved-out mouth, three small white stones had been wedged. It had painted stripes — brown, yellow, and black — for eyebrows. When Charles shook it, the dried coconut, hard as a stone, "boomed," sounding like a drum beat, not maracas.

"It's just, well, it's just not what I was expecting," Max said, catching his breath.

"It's really old. Someone's souvenir from some tropical place."

"Maybe Florida. Maybe from one of those scary shops down on the Ocean City Boardwalk."

"Shall I bring him with me?" Charles asked in a wishing voice.

"No! Well, maybe you can talk to Grandma and tell her you found it. Let her decide," Max said. He didn't want it hanging around in their room at home. He suspected if Charles did take it, that's exactly what he would do, place it someplace in their room where Max would have to see it all the time. *'Nope, that's not going to happen.'*

"Did you find the comforters? Are they in that trunk, too?"

"Yep, Mr. Coconut Man must have been guarding them. Keeping them safe from rats and mice and things that go crawling into hidden little openings in steamer trunks."

"I doubt it. OK, put Coconut Man down. Pull the comforters out, then return him to the trunk for safekeeping and let's get on with this project."

Charles did as he was told. He began hauling out the comforters. "Here they are — whew! Mothballs. We have to get a move on and let them air or I'll be . . . A-a-achoo! Sneezing all night."

"Can you get two out or do you need some help?" Max asked. He was really scared of going where Charles was because it meant being an excellent balance-beam walker, something he wasn't very good at. In school he always had to jump quickly off after only one or two steps.

"Achoooo!! Got one," Charles pulled a comforter out, reached in and pulled out another. "Whew! They're big and stinky. Achoooo!" He closed the lid.

"Here, I'll come as far as this door. Can you get them that close to me? Good. I'll pull them the rest of the way, one at a time."

They had gotten both comforters to the top of the stairs. They already had the duffle bag there, so all they had to do was let the stuff roll. They were just about to when two things happened, or maybe it was only one, but . . .

At the same time, two flashlights and a light bulb went out.

At the same time, Max was sure he saw a curtain bag sway.

At the same time, he was sure the wader boots had begun swinging by themselves, with their feet looking as if they were taking big footsteps.

At the same time, just as the screams began to move from their toes to their tongues then out their lips . . .

. . . the attic door opened wide and they heard a voice:

"Boys, are you all right?"

The light overhead beamed bright.

Both flashlights simultaneously went back on and were as bright as spotlights. The waders stopped swinging and their feet sat motionless.

The voice at the bottom of the stairs they recognized as their own Grandma.

"Ohhhhh!"

"Whew!!!!"

"Achooo!"

"Max? Charles?"

"We're here, Grandma, and we found both the comforters and the tent."

"They're all here at the top of the steps."

"Wonderful! Push the tent first, let it slide down the stairs," Grandma said. She applauded them. "Good job. Grandpa will be proud, too."

"Achooo! Achooo! Yes ma'am!" Charles said, wiping his dripping nose on the bottom of his T-shirt.

Max pushed the duffle bag and watched it roll like any tightly packed bag. "Thump-plump-thumpity-thump-plump," to the very bottom. Grandma pushed it aside with her feet. "Now those stinky comforters," she said.

Max pulled the heavy feather comforters away from Charles.

Charles gladly moved away from them.

Max pushed them.

They slipped, slid, slopped, stopped.

Max stepped down a few steps and kicked them again.

They lumped, bumped, slumped, twisted, turned, tumbled, softly, slowly, step-by-step, down the stairs. At the bottom, Grandma snatched them up, squished and rolled them into two small balls. She was a pro at handling bedclothes.

"Come down, boys. You need to get out of the dust, dirt, and staleness of clutter. You need something cold to drink and we need to air these comforters. Whew! Smells like someone must have had a personal investment in saving comforters from nibbling bad inNESTors like furry rodents and flying moths!"

Grandma, like Grandpa, enjoyed words and word plays.

"I'll meet you two outside. Grandpa is ready to work on the tent, but be sure to get a cold drink before you come out to help," Grandma called over her shoulder. She'd already left the Museum and was hurrying down to the first floor.

Chapter 8

Setting up the Tent, Comforters Airing, Free Time

At each end of the duffle bag were worn leather, soft-as-cloth handles. Max took one, Charles the other.

"One. Two. Three." They picked it up.

The duffle was more cumbersome than heavy. Its awkward weight waddled as they lugged it through the Museum. They were especially careful not to knock into any furniture. Most particularly they stepped far away from Great-Grandma's favorite rocking chair. On full-moon nights, it was known to start rocking without anyone in or near it. "Squeeeeeak-squeeeeak."

Grandma and Grandpa always told the boys "not to worry about this spirit. She's sweet and only returns to rock the babies she gave birth to but which never lived."

"If they had lived, I would have had more brothers and

sisters, but such were the times back then," Grandpa had once said.

At the steps to the downstairs, Max and Charles let go and gave a push. The duffle rolled down the steps. They carried it into the kitchen and plopped it down. On the kitchen table was a sign drawn in Grandma's script: "Max and Charles, Drink Me!" Behind it were two glasses of ice-cold lemonade.

"Oh, Grandma, wherever you are right now, thanks," Max said.

The boys drank it so quickly they hardly tasted the spicy fresh mint.

Refreshed, they hoisted the duffle bag, managing not to knock it against furniture, windows, or doorjambs. They lugged it through narrow openings, then dropped it onto the cement porch. Fitzgerald immediately came to greet them, but seeing the duffle, she stepped back and started growling.

"It's OK, Fitz, it's only an old tent."

Fitz sniffed, nudged, then climbed on top of it. She made three turns and curled on it as if it were her new bed.

Charles and Max laughed.

They rubbed and patted her spotted sides and scratched behind her silky black ears. "Silly dog."

In the backyard they saw Grandma had already hung one comforter on the clothesline and was tossing the second one up and on. As soon as she had it in place, she picked up an old-fashioned rug beater and began whacking it as hard as she could. She was smacking out mothball smells and smashing in fresh air.

Grandpa came from the garage to the porch riding on his little green and yellow tractor with black cart attached. He parked, put it in neutral, set the brake, and shut off the purring engine. He swung one leg over and slid off the bright yellow seat like a child sliding off a sliding board, then walked to the edge of the cement porch.

"Whatcha got there? Ah, yes, good job! My old duffle and inside of it the tent and I bet you found it somewhere in the darkest part of the attic."

Max turned to a drippy Charles and gave him a high-five.

"We survived the Attic," Max said.

"Yeah," Charles said with a loud sniff, followed by another "Achooo!"

"Mothball smells don't agree with Charles," Grandma said, beating the comforters.

"I can sympathize with that. But by bedtime, they'll smell just fine," Grandpa reassured them. He climbed the steps onto the porch, knelt on one knee, and began the task of unlatching all the leather and belt-buckle straps. At last, with the help of Max and Charles, all were undone. He flipped back the flaps and there was a mustard-brown, World War II-vintage, canvas tent.

"Max, grab hold of the back end of the duffle bag. Charles, help me pull the tent out. It's been 'duffled' snug as a bug in a rug for a long, long time, ever since your Mom was a little girl."

"That's a long time ago," Charles said.

Max gave him a dirty look.

"I mean . . . it hasn't been used since before Max was born," Charles said, verbally back-pedaling.

"No, it hasn't. Probably not since your Mom was nineteen or twenty."

"A very long time," Charles blurted.

"You're telling me?" Grandpa asked. Then he laughed. "OK, back to work."

It took a lot of muscle and pulling, but finally the tent was out. It looked like a long, thick caterpillar resting on the grass. Now the job was to untie ropes and unfold it. Then, like the comforters, it would hang on the clothesline.

"I think we need to let it air on the line for a couple of hours, then we'll take it to your campsite in the back here," Grandpa pointed to the cart hitched to his mower.

Getting the two-man tent onto the clothesline was a four-person task. It was heavy, it was awkward, and as Grandpa said: "It has a mind all its own." After it was finally on the line, they had to fiddle with it to "make sure as much air can flow in as possible," he said.

"And now, boys," Grandma said. "Free time. Time for you two to go off and play. You've been working hard and doing good work, but it's Saturday. Scoot! And don't let me see you doing any work until it's time to pitch that tent and fix your bed things. Charles, what time do you have?"

Charles reported, "1:30."

Grandpa pulled his gold pocket watch out from his watch pocket and popped open its little protective door. "1:30 it is."

"Good. Report back here at 4. What do you think, Grandpa?"

"Sounds good. We shouldn't need more than 45 minutes to get it set up for the night."

"Wash-up is 4:45. Dinner at 5:00," Grandma said. "Now scoot!"

Max and Charles looked at each other, wondering what to do first. They were hot, they were dirty, they wanted to . . .

"Let's go swim," Max said.

"Yeah!" Charles agreed.

"Perfect idea," said Grandpa.

"And I have extra clothes for you when you're cleaner than you are now," said Grandma.

The boys bolted for the best swimming on the Property: the big stream by the farm pond and beside the giant willow.

Fitz started to follow but Grandpa whistled her back. Tail drooping, she obeyed him. Yappy, startled from his afternoon nap, howled twice, then circled three times and settled back to catch his dreams again, resting on his favorite place on the roof of his house.

The boys ran across the parking area, through the long field grass, to the big vegetable and berry garden. It was early in the season, only May 1, but perhaps they could find a few ripe strawberries. It was worth a try.

They divided up, each taking a row. Carefully they turned over dark green leaves in search of afternoon-warmed, juicy-ripe strawberries.

"Here's one. Oh, never mind. A turtle took a bite out of the ripe part of it."

"I have one. It has a white tip but . . . "

"That's not ripe!"

"I'm taking it anyway. Yum." Max sucked on the berry, letting the sweet, warm juice swish in his mouth for as long as he could before swallowed. Even though it was not fully ripe, it was better than what the stores were selling from far away.

"Here's one. Oh wow. So good," Charles cooed. He'd finally found a fully ripe berry.

"OK, we stop at five each. And we must report to Grandma that a few are ripe," Max said.

"Do we have to tell her we picked and ate five each?" Charles asked.

"No, I don't think so, not unless she asks. But I bet she won't. Grandma understands. She used to pick strawberries when she was growing up on a farm."

"And Grandpa?"

"Are you kidding? Grandpa not understand a boy's need to eat homegrown strawberries?"

"Yeah, you're right," Charles said. "Oh, here's another. That makes two."

"And I have three more. Meet you at the pond when you have your five."

Sitting in the unmown, dark-green grass inches from new cattail leaves growing beside old stems, listening to the "pluck" when small frogs popped in, two barefoot boys slowly ate their strawberries.

"This is our reward, Charles," Max said thoughtfully.

"Yeah, I hope this good luck feeling stays and doesn't leave us when we're on watch duty in that tent," Charles said.

"I know, it might be scary, but you and I know Grandma and Grandpa aren't going to put our lives in danger. You must believe it is for our education. It's their way of teaching us something important; something important we will always remember," Max said.

"You really believe that?"

"I have to or I'd be scared crazy over what they want us to do tonight," Max said. He finished his last strawberry and slid from sitting down into rolling onto his back. He looked up at the sky. "Red skies in the morning, sailor's warning . . ."

"Red skies this morning at sunrise, remember?"

"I do. But so far the sky is blue and I don't see one cloud. I guess not every old saying is true."

"Hope not," Charles said. He was on his belly now, "squinching" his way closer and closer to the pond.

"Frogging?" Max said

"Yep."

"See any?"

"Not yet."

Max rolled over. He lowered his head until his pointy chin was plowing the ground. He nosed his way closer and closer to the pond's edge using his elbows to pull and his toes to push. Close enough, he stopped and waited.

One minute, two minutes passed, then he saw a frog, but not just any frog: bullfrog. He was sure. He knew he couldn't make a sound or he might frighten the monster amphibian. It was only about twelve inches from him.

The bullfrog hovered high in the mix of pond slime, weeds, twigs, and water. His olive green back shown in the sun, while his brownish side markings and white belly were hidden by the water. His upper lip was bright green, throat yellow. And Max thought, *'big eyes like the wolf in Little Red Riding Hood.'* The bullfrog's brown irises and almond-shaped pupils looked huge. *'He's waiting, but for what?'* Max wondered.

Then he saw the prey: a miniature crayfish with its back to the pond, feelers stretching, claws waving *'at . . . at what? Oh, gosh, at me,'* Max realized.

The crayfish was between Max and the bullfrog. All of its concentration was focused on big, threatening Max. *'Big mistake,'* Max thought as he watched the bullfrog make his move.

Powerful jaws open, tiny teeth grasped the back fins of the crayfish's tail. Before the crayfish could turn and attack with small pinching jaws, the bullfrog's mucus-coated tongue engulfed it. In an instant the big white jaws clamped down. The crayfish disappeared.

'What next?' Max closed his eyes. Eye-witnessing the food chain was harder when the live action was right in front of you, not shown on TV with ten commercial breaks.

"Oh, oh," Max moaned.

The bullfrog heard him. A tremendous "whoosh . . . splash" as it dove down and away.

"What's the matter with you?" Charles asked.

"I've just witnessed a murder," Max moaned.

"Murder? Where? Here? What?" He rolled over until he was right beside his older brother.

"Take it from me, Charles, you don't want to know."

"No? Know not ever?"

"No, know not yet. Maybe when you're older . . . maybe then I'll be able to re-view the scene again as I describe it."

"Oh, OK. Ah, so it was like nightmare material?"

"Yeah. I think at eight you should still have happy dreams."

"OK, how about NOW we go swimming in the Big Stream?"

"Good idea," said Max, opening his eyes. He rolled over and stood, then made six broad-jump leaps to the bank of the stream. Charles was beside him in mini-minutes.

The Big Stream began as a tiny spring bubbling free from a hidden aquifer, deep beneath the ground. It meandered through acres of hardwoods: oaks, maples, black walnuts, beech. It twisted like a snake sunning itself on a rock. It pooled beside the places where once American chestnuts towered, before the fungus began to spread, wiping out millions of trees by 1940.

In valleys, the stream paralleled hillsides with silvered rails of a fence built during the Civil War. Sometimes it flowed as a small brook, a crooked path of water; sometimes it was wide as if imitating a river. More often, especially during years of no rain, it was reduced to a trickle far away from any roads or even horse trails.

By the time the stream edged the pony pasture and garden of the Property, it was a strong healthy stream with pools deep enough for hiding trout and welcoming children to wade, float, even doggie paddle in.

After passing by the farm pond where Max's bullfrog

encounter had occurred, and not far from Grandma and Grandpa's garden, the Big Stream plunged noisily into the ribbed hollows of a metal culvert, echoing loud splashes and tumbling roars. It tunneled under a country road and into an abandoned horse farm. A few miles later it joined with other streams and somewhere hidden, miles away, it became part of a river.

During bad rainstorms or hurricanes, Big Stream swelled and was dangerous. One summer, after a hurricane, the boys watched as it conquered its banks, joining with the farm pond. High, flooding water, pond and stream together, churned across the pasture and gardens, lake-like in size, wild like whitewater. It slapped and rippled until, within a few hundred feet of their grandparents' house, it slowed into muddy brown, harmless suds.

On this May 1, the stream was only halfway up its banks: two feet deep on one side of the sandbar island, four feet on the other side, forming a perfect swimming hole for two sweaty boys.

Max and Charles yanked off shoes, wiggled out of T-shirts, shorts, stripped down to briefs, and slid down the thick, green, grassy bank and into cool, cool water.

"Ah!"

"Reward at last!" Charles yelled. He splashed through the shallows, crossed the sandbar, and entered shadowy darkness made by overhanging willow boughs. "Ah," he said, then made a shallow, dive-like lunge. He swam underwater, his body swishing back and forth like a river otter. He "hand-walked" on the bottom. When he surfaced, his hair was plastered over his eyes as water streamed down to his lips and into his open mouth. He sputtered, then yelled: "Perrrr-fection!"

Of the two boys, he was the swimmer. He was on the school's team from late August, when practices began, until June of the next year. Summers found him at the swim club near their home, practicing his favorite stroke, the butterfly, and competing in his second favorite, but his best so far: the crawl.

Max stone-hopped through the shallows to "Sandbar Island," as he liked to call it. The sandbar split the stream into two parts: on one side a swimming hole where Charles was acting like a cross between a freshwater otter and a huge trout; on the other, shallow but fast-moving current, rippling around large quartz stones, spinning leaves, pushing sticks and fallen branches of an apple tree to create a partial dam.

The sandbar was soft sand mixed with silt and sparkling tiny flakes of mica. Max sat down here and dangled his feet in the cold water. He cupped his hands, dipped them into the steam, filled them, then splashed his face and head. "Ah!" It felt good to be cooled off and cleaner.

Max had no plans to wade, float, or go snorkeling without a snorkel like Charles. Max had his own plan. From the shallows he gathered tiny pebbles, collecting two handfuls of rounded and jagged brown, white, and rosy quartz and placed them in a pile. Next he shifted on the sand until he was closer to the stream bank. He leaned over, elbows on his knees, and reached under the overhanging sod and long thick grasses of the bank. He dug until he had all he needed, then pulled his hand back. His palm was filled with gray clay. The same kind of gray clay Native Americans used, hundreds of years ago, to make soapstone pottery. Max put his handful down. If he needed more he knew where he could get it. If he had more than he needed, he knew where to return it. He looked around and finally found a large, almost-flat piece of birch bark that had washed downstream and been stopped by the dam. *'Perfect,'* Max thought.

On the birch bark, Max began building a miniature house using the clay and stones. First he rolled pinches of clay from the bulk between his palms into four, two-inch-long pieces. Next he placed them on the bark in a square: The foundation. He left an opening for a door. He selected certain stones and pushed them into the clay. *'And the walls go up.'* Clay, stones, clay, stones, up and up. "I'm building a little house the way Grandma showed me," he whispered to himself.

When the stone house was about two inches high, Max gathered little sticks which had fallen into the stream, floated, and become lodged along the bank. He broke them into equal lengths, each three inches. One by one he pushed each into the top layer of clay, side touching side.

'Not a house yet, looks like a clay and stone box,' he thought. *'This will be the tough part.'* He needed to cut out one or two windows. He decided it was something he'd need Grandma or Grandpa's help with. He stood, bent over, and carefully picked it up. He carried the bark with his little building on it and placed it where he felt it

would be safe, between the black walnut tree's large, knobby roots. He'd leave it there until he was ready. He looked up into the tree limbs to see — and yes, there it was — a nest he looked for every year since Grandpa showed him, the stocking-like nest of a Baltimore oriole.

Now it was time to wash off clay and see what stream creatures he could find downstream, away from where Charles was swimming. Maybe later he could get Charles to go with him in the tunnel. A scary place.

He sat on the sandbar and stared into the flowing water. Yes, some minnows. They were the size of the fish in Grandpa's aquarium. "Little silvery flickering, flashing, flighty fish fleets, flamboyant finning finery," Max whispered, practicing his tongue-twisting skills. Nearby, he spied two crayfish in a standoff, dueling position: claws opening and clenching closed, opening and closing. "Good thing for you guys Mr. Bullfrog is not around," Max said in a voice Charles could not hear.

Meanwhile, Charles was grabbing willow strands, gripping them high, pushing off from the stream bank, swinging out, and practicing his splashdowns.

The afternoon moved on, each boy doing what he loved to do.

Then they heard noises.

Fitz and Yappy barking.

A car, loud, louder as it came around the twisty driveway, silence when the motor was turned off. Doors shutting, sounds of voices calling, greeting each other. After a few minutes the dogs stopped barking. The boys heard no more voices. And then voices again, coming from the house towards the farm pond.

"We'd better grab our clothes and hide," Max said. The fear of being caught in only briefs made all other thoughts leave his mind.

Both boys splashed through the stream, grabbed clothes and shoes, then waded back across the water and ducked under the long-leafed boughs of the Mighty Willow. They went as far back as possible, backs against its gray bark.

The Mighty Willow was the biggest tree on the Property. It was tall and wide as a playhouse. Under its curtain of drooping, lacy branches, the boys could hide and believe they'd never be found; its long, streaming boughs hung down, ends touching the water when it was stirred.

From this hiding place, their camouflaged "fort," Max and Charles often peered out to spy on anyone working in Grandma and Grandpa's garden or those who visited Grandpa at the farm pond to learn the art of casting with a fly rod.

"Hey look, it's Pat and Mrs. Sullivan!"

Pat was a tall, willowy Irishman, former high school cross-country runner, Eagle Scout, now Appalachian Trail hiker, rustic-style camper. His hair was blond and cut (by his wife) in a mid-1980s flop-to-his-shoulders style. His bony, rosy face boasted a bushy mustache. His huge sea-sky blue eyes were enlarged by gold-rimmed, granny-type glasses with thick lenses. His smile was that of a shy guy, but he was more laid-back than shy, letting children/teens/adults come to him. He would always be there to help but he'd never force any issue. He was a great listener, which was perfect, because his beloved wife, Mrs. Sullivan, was an entertaining, extraordinary storyteller and very different from Pat in many ways.

Mrs. Sullivan was Greek. Her nickname was *Popie* (pronounced "Pope–ee"), which translated into English as "beautiful voice." She had enormous dark brown, comforting eyes which sparkled when she was laughing, excited, or thrilled for one of her students. Her hair was a mass of thick curls which always had their own way. She was soft, not fat, with muscular arms as strong as Pat's.

Both Pat and Popie were teachers.

No matter the occasion, Pat was usually dressed in blue jeans, clean when he needed to be well-dressed. He wore T-shirts from music festivals, souvenirs from a wide range of places. Some of his tees showed classic ads from long ago, others had handsome logos. A few were from political campaigns. When truly dressed up, Pat wore a collared dress shirt, sleeves rolled at the elbows, front-buttoned half-way, shirttail out.

No matter the occasion, Mrs. Sullivan wore bright flowered blouses or dresses often trimmed in white cotton, crocheted or tatted collars, some jewelry, and dressy but sensible shoes.

The boys always called them Pat and Mrs. Sullivan. She was their mom's best friend. And now she and Pat were also best friends with Fred.

Pat often helped Grandma and Grandpa with the garden. He also grew vegetables and melons on the Property different from what Grandpa usually grew. Pat liked to experiment and had grown Korean melons, spaghetti squash, Jerusalem artichokes, bok choy, hot Asian radishes, and all kinds of peppers. Pat gave a share to Grandma and Grandpa, and sometimes the next year, Grandpa would try growing one of Pat's vegetable varieties.

Other than certain family members, Pat and Mrs. Sullivan were Max and Charles' favorite grownups. Pat was an artistic woodworker, creating furniture from trees he found or people gave him. Recently someone cleared a dense woodlot to build a house, and their contractor called Pat, offering him huge oak and maple logs if he'd come and get them. Pat made many trips, rolling the logs up ramps and into the bed of his pickup, then taking them to his shop. He told Grandpa and the boys about a new saw he'd bought that sliced wood length-wise to reveal "not yearly tree rings, but the core, which is called heartwood. It looks like a river flowing down the middle of the tree," Pat said. "I've been working weeks on this hobby. Out of one log I've made four coffee tables. Now, I have to figure out how to market them."

Mrs. Sullivan was a third-grade teacher. Every kindergarten, first- and second-grade student and their parents adored her. No third-grader wanted to leave her classroom. When former students were in high school, college and beyond, they still stopped in at recess or wrote her notes. Max and Charles didn't attend the school where she taught, but they knew students who did. At first they wished she was their teacher, but then decided it was best to have her in their lives as their mom's best friend.

Max and Charles looked through the willow boughs.

Pat was in the garden using Grandpa's old-fashioned, hand-push cultivator, working the soil soft.

"Mrs. Sullivan's here to take casting lessons from Grandpa. See? They're walking down to the pond. Grandpa has two fly rods in his hand. He's going to teach her how to be a great fly fisherwoman," Max whispered to Charles.

"And I bet she will be," Charles whispered back.

"Grandpa's really a famous fly fisherman. He's made the cover of *Field & Stream* and been in lots of fishing stories. Mom says when she was little, there were always young guys, men, some girls, and women, too, like Mrs. Sullivan, coming here to learn fly-fishing from him. You know, like he shows us: how to 'feed out' then 'slide in' a line. I wonder what he'll be teaching Mrs. Sullivan? And I wonder how she'll do?"

"I bet she'll do fantastic. And Grandpa will give her an A."

The boys moved closer and jockeyed for better views without being seen. They watched Grandpa demonstrate how to cast by making loops like a cowboy's rope spins before he lassoes a steer.

"It's all in the wrist," they overheard Grandpa say. "Here, hold your pocketbook against your side with your elbow. Now cast. If your pocketbook falls, we'll know you're using your arm and not your wrist."

The boys watched Mrs. Sullivan try. They saw her pocketbook fall, "clump" onto the ground.

"Ah, a miss," Charles sighed.

"Hey, give her a break. That was her first try."

"I'm so sorry. I guess I didn't trust my wrist," Mrs. Sullivan said, loud enough for them to hear. She picked her pocketbook up and put it back next to her ribs. "I'll try to do better this time," she said with one of her big smiles.

"No problem," Grandpa said. "It's hard to do in the beginning."

After several tries and several pocketbook plops, Mrs. Sullivan got it.

"There you go. Good. Now, I want you to aim the fly so it almost touches the water. But don't let it touch the water. Pull in your line before it breaks the surface. Bring it back. Let out more line, more line. Make the loop bigger, careful, careful . . . Good! That's it. Now, on this cast softly let your fly drop onto the pond's surface. Oops, pocketbook just fell again. But you're making great progress."

Max and Charles knew how hard it was to cast a fly line the right way. Grandpa had been schooling them ever since they were toddlers. He'd made them each small bamboo rods with their names inscribed in Grandma's fine penmanship, then covered by many layers of varnish. They practiced for hours on the pond's still water.

The pond was not a trout pond. The springs feeding it were too weak. Additional water flowed in from the Big Stream through a buried plastic pipe. But still the water was too warm, green algae grew, and the bottom was mucky mud. Blue gills, carp, sunfish and frogs thrived, but not trout.

Max and Charles became experts at casting on the farm

pond, where trees were far away and there were only summer cattails to get hung up in. But when Grandpa took them fishing at Hunting Creek, one of the streams stocked with their hatchery trout, casting was no longer easy. Both Max and Charles spent most of their fishing time not casting or fishing but trying to get their beautiful homemade flies out of tree branches and tight rock jams. Not fun.

After eavesdropping on the casting lesson for a few minutes, Max and Charles both leaned back against the Mighty Willow and rested. It was only 3:00, but it had already been a long day. They both wondered what the evening would be like. Neither wanted to discuss it. Both wanted to appear brave.

The sun was as warm as a June day. The air was still, and honeysuckle, wild rose, and catawba blossoms blended into a sweet and comforting fragrance.

"I never smelled anything as good as this. Have you?" Charles said to Max.

"Nope. Not even when Mom or Grandma bake, it never smells as good as this."

"Nope, never."

Moments passed, then Max noticed voices were fading and beside him it was really quiet. He looked over and saw Charles had fallen asleep. Slowly and as carefully as he could, Max bent forward and moved a few willow boughs so he could see out again. He saw Grandpa, Mrs. Sullivan, and Pat walking away. He guessed maybe they were going to visit with Grandma at the house. Now might be a good time to dress and leave their hiding place. There was still time to do other things he knew Charles wanted to do before going back to work. He nudged Charles.

"Whaaaa?"

"We can get dressed and escape now. Grandpa, Pat, and Mrs. Sullivan are headed to the house."

"Ah, OK," Charles yawned, then stretched. "You got a plan to do something new?"

"Yep." Max had on his T-shirt and was pulling on his shorts.

"What?" Charles picked up his shorts and wiggled them on without standing.

"Rope swing," Max said. He picked up his shoes by their long, grungy laces.

"Oh, yeah!" Charles squirmed into his T-shirt and knotted the laces of his shoes around his wrist (he was afraid he'd lose his grip on them and they'd fall in the Big Stream). "Good plan."

Max led the way, re-crossing the stream stones he'd used before. Both boys scrambled up the stream bank.

"Meet you there!" Charles yelled over his shoulder. He dashed ahead.

'Good,' Max thought. He went to the black walnut tree, stopped, looked for and soon found his stone, clay, and twig "house" between the roots where he'd left it. 'I need to put this in the barn someplace safe.' He had to walk slowly so the little clay house wouldn't begin to lean to one side or, even worse, collapse on its birch-bark foundation.

He didn't have to carry it too far. At the edge of the

garden he saw an empty cardboard box. *'Maybe Pat brought something and planted it today.'* Max put his creation in it. It was a perfect fit. He closed the four flaps and carried the box to the pony barn, where he put it in the back where Grandpa's worktable was. On top of the table there was plenty of room. Then Max ran to join Charles at the rope swing.

Chapter 9

Rope Swing and Then . . .

Max and Charles had plenty of games, but one they loved to play didn't come in a box, wasn't fancy, and wasn't bought in a toy store. The Rope Swing was their favorite game. It was hemp rope that their uncle, Fred, and Grandpa hung high on an oak limb, not far from their grandparents' sleeping-porch, and beside a trickling steam.

"Best fun kids ever have is a rope swing tied to a high, strong limb," Grandpa told many parents. Some believed him. Some didn't.

★★★★★

When each boy turned eight, they were taught how to climb a rope the easy way: grab hold of the first big knot tied in the rope, grasp the bottom of the rope with your feet, one foot on top of the other, with rope caught in between. To go higher, reach for the next knot, let feet swing free, clamp rope with feet again. Up, up, up high as you dared.

"When you're a teen," Grandpa said, "we'll teach you to climb a rope without using your feet. Right, Fred?"

Max and Charles loved watching Fred's face turn red, hearing him sputter, and then admit, "I'm out of practice doing it the hard way. Guess I'll have to start exercising and getting in better shape."

"Two more years, Fred," Grandpa reminded him, "then Max will be a teen. Thirteen. But then again, I'm forgetting Ralph. You need to shape up now as he's been a teen for three years."

"Yes, sir," Fred said sheepishly.

Being Fred, he began immediately practicing. And before this day in May, actually during the first week of April, he was in shape and showed the boys how to climb a rope using only hands, feet swinging freely.

"Immmmmm-presssss-ive!" Charles had yelled.

Max beamed a big smile and clapped. "Knew you could do it, Fred, proud of you."

★★★★★

"Hey, what took you so long?" Charles called when Max appeared.

"Had to . . . you know, bathroom."

"Oh, yeah. OK. I was getting worried you'd forgotten the way here . . . or worse, gotten stolen by the one who's taking Grandpa's fish."

"Not to worry. Have you started yet? Is it my turn now?"

"No, I was waiting for you to get here. In case I did something an audience should see."

'Oh, boy,' thought Max, *'one power nap and now Charles is full of himself.'* Aloud he said, "OK. I'm ready, show me."

Charles took the end of the hemp rope. He wrapped it around the tree trunk half-way. Put his hands up to the first knot on the rope.

"Ready? Watching?" he called to Max.

"Yep. Want me to count you down?"

"Sure," Charles said and placed one foot on the trunk of the tree.

"OK. Ready . . ."

Charles slid his foot higher up the trunk.

"Set."

Charles moved his other foot from ground to tree trunk.

"Go!" Max said in a whisper.

Charles slid his feet side by side and then pushed off. He swung out and towards the little stream and then jumped off.

Max applauded.

Charles bowed.

"My turn?"

"Sure, and I'll count *you* down."

Max took the rope from Charles, wrapped it around the tree trunk, but further around than Charles had, his hands went to the next knot on the rope. "OK, Charles, do your countdown," he said.

"One for the money."

"A Grandpa countdown. Good for you." Max slid his feet to the base of the tree, put both together, heels touching.

"Two for the show," Charles said dramatically.

Max took a hop onto the trunk.

"Three to get rrreaaddddy," Charles dragged it out.

Max hopped two more times up the trunk, holding the rope at arms' length.

"And four to . . . GO!!!!"

Max pushed off the tree trunk, he swung around, passing close to the stream. He was going fast, looping out and around, then looping towards the trunk again, but from the opposite side, his knees up and feet side-by-side, heels together. He let the rope wrap around the tree as far as it would, feet connected with trunk, and he kicked off a second time, again swinging out and looping round, but this time he let go and jumped before the rope had come too close to the tree.

"Cool! Wowee!" yelled Charles.

Max smiled and took a bow.

"Who taught you how to do that?"

"How much is it worth to you?" Max winked his eye, raised one brow and looked smug.

Charles knew Max was imitating him when he got all full of himself. "OK, Max, I get it. But honestly, who showed you how to do that rope trick? It's really cool."

"Variations on a swing," Max said. "Actually, one day when you were away at some doctor or dentist check-up thing, I was down here fooling around and came up with

. . . as I just said: Variations on a Swing. It's fun. You have to be careful, though. You can scrape your knees really easily. And landing's not something to take lightly."

"Will you teach me?" Charles said.

"Sure."

Time flew as they practiced.

"Hey Charles, what time is it?"

"Ah, let me check."

When they went from the garden to the Big Stream, Charles had taken off his watch and buttoned it into one of the many pockets on his shorts. He hadn't looked or thought about time since. He felt the outside of his shorts, found the pocket and unbuttoned it.

"Hey, Max, it's 3:45," he said in a surprised voice. "How could it get so late so fast"

"Time goes by when you're at Grandma and Grandpa's house," Max said. "Time to meet Grandpa and get that tent."

"Time for one last swing?"

"Sure, go ahead, but be careful. Always respect the rope."

"I do. And I will," Charles said, and he did. He was careful. He took one last swing, kicking off perfectly and landing on his feet with no slip.

"Dare I say it . . . perfect takeoff, perfect landing. You did it so . . . so gracefully," Max said. He was proud at how seriously Charles played on the rope swing.

They walked to the backyard. No clothes on the clothesline. No comforters. And no tent. They looked at each other. They were halfway to the cement porch when they noticed two things. Grandpa's tractor with cart was not there, and parked beside Grandma's car and Grandpa's truck was Pat's truck.

"Hey, I wonder what's going on," Charles said.

"I don't know. Things are different from the plan. I guess we better go in and find out what's going on," Max said.

Chapter 10

Dinner Guests? You Bet

Max and Charles entered the house through the back door of the glassed-in porch and into the kitchen. They were greeted with some of their favorite cooking smells, but no Grandma, no Grandpa, no Fitzgerald, no Pat, and no Mrs. Sullivan. Max looked in the dining room.

"Hey, Charles, come here."

Charles looked, "Wow, Grandma's very best and it's not Thanksgiving, Christmas, or Easter. Is it an important birthday?"

"I don't know," Max said. "The table is set for six: Grandma, Grandpa … and four dinner guests?"

The boys listened but the only sound in the whole house was water bubbling in the fish aquarium and the ticking of Great-Grandmother's clock on the fireplace mantel.

"I guess everyone's outside. Let's check places we didn't

go near on our way back here," Max said. He led the way to the back door.

Outside again and listening now, they faintly heard voices coming from the Big Spring and field beyond.

"Let's go see what's going on," Max said.

They ran past Trout Pools #1 and #2 to the Big Spring. The voices were louder, but the boys didn't see anything. Then, looking around near the spring, but to the pasture by a grove of tall red cedars and old, bushy, long-needled pine trees, Charles said, "There they are."

The boys ran to the adults.

Fitzgerald heard them and began barking. Soon she was running around them with her tail flagging as fast as a window fan.

"Hi!" Grandma called. "Come see who's here. And do we have surprises for you."

"Max and Charles!" Mrs. Sullivan put out her arms, offering a hug. Both boys hugged Mrs. Sullivan at the same time. She was just like a mom to them. They shook hands with Pat.

"Good to see you guys again. Been growing, I see," Pat said.

"Yes, sir. Max is 'moving on up,'" Charles said, "but I have a bigger shoe size."

Max looked at Grandpa who was sitting on the yellow seat of his riding mower. Grandpa gave him a thumb's up. 'Huh?' Max thought. He looked at the little cart hooked behind the tractor. It was empty.

"So, I'm suspecting you kiddos are wondering what's going on," Grandma said.

"Sort-of, kind-of," Charles said.

"Well, I didn't tell you, but Grandpa and I invited Pat and Mrs. Sullivan here today. Some gardening needed to be done, which Pat graciously did. Mrs. Sullivan had a fly-casting lesson with Grandpa."

"Which he so patiently gave me, putting up with my not wanting to do it the way it's supposed to be done," said Mrs. Sullivan. She looked over to Grandpa and grinned.

"It's all in the wrist," he said with a laugh.

"So I'm learning. You know, you never stop learning," Mrs. Sullivan said.

"And the rest of the plan is they're staying for dinner. And so are you two, once you clean up. Not to worry. I have clothes set out for you both in the spare bedroom. But you are both to shower first, and that's an order," Grandma said.

"Yes, ma'am. We will. But . . ." Max began.

"You're wondering about the tent and the comforters? Come here," Grandpa said.

Max and Charles went to where Grandpa was. They stood beside the mower. He pointed to the bushy pines. They moved closer. Pat stepped ahead of them and with one long, strong arm pushed pine boughs back. He held the branches with his tough, woodworker's hand. Then they saw the tent. It was set up. Inside of it they could see the comforters.

"Since I was here and I have a little more muscle than you guys, not that you won't when you're as old as me, I told your grandpa I'd help you," Pat said.

"Oh, wow, thank you, Pat!" Max said.

Max and Charles ducked into the pine grove surrounding the tent. It was small but big enough to fit chairs and other things; it was like a little room. They explored the tent. The comforters smelled fresh. Charles didn't start sneezing. A real thumbs up. It was perfect and hidden. If the fish thief came back tonight, there was no way he'd see their campsite.

"Well, it's a good place to be. Hidden but close to the Big Spring," Grandpa said.

"Yeah," Max and Charles agreed.

"OK, boys, cleanup time. We'll meet you in the living room at, oh, let's say 4:45," Grandma said. "Dinner will still be at 5:00, but since it's special, we'll have appetizers."

"It's special having Pat and Mrs. Sullivan here," Max said.

"Oh, Max, how kind," Mrs. Sullivan smiled. When she smiled her whole face smiled, and it seemed like her whole body smiled, too.

'She's the living expression of all smiles,' Max thought.

"Well, it's a special day for me, and your grandparents are making it even more special," Mrs. Sullivan continued. "Really?" Charles asked.

"Really, Charles. Today is my birthday and I'm celebrating it with you. The first plan was to celebrate by going out with your Mom, Fred, and Pat. But then your mom got a call from an old, old friend, Lise, who lives far away in Alaska. Lise was traveling back home from visiting family in France and there was a weather delay, an overnight at BWI Airport. She has never seen your sister Carrie."

"Wow. Carrie is over a year old now!" Charles exclaimed.

"Yes, so it was really a wonderful opportunity for your Mom and Fred to show off their little one. It was very sudden and unexpected and . . . well, a big change of plans."

"But it'll be grand," Pat said. He reached down and gave her a hug.

"Do you know what?" Grandma said.

"What?" Charles and Max said at the same time.

"Mrs. Sullivan brought her own special birthday dessert. And I made something special too, so we'll have not one but . . ."

"Actually, I couldn't decide and brought several. So we'll have lots of dessert," Mrs. Sullivan laughed. "You boys don't mind?"

"Yum!" Charles said.

"Yes, very yum. But now, boys, you must hurry and get cleaned up," Grandma told them.

"Off we go!" Charles sprinted ahead.

"See you when we're clean again," Max said.

"Later," said Pat.

"See you soon," Mrs. Sullivan added.

"Scrub!" called Grandma.

"Toodle-le-doo!" Grandpa said. It was his favorite expression for "goodbye for now".

'Now I know why I made the little miniature house. And I know who I'm giving it to,' Max thought as he loped back towards the house. On his way he thought, *'I'll swing into the barn and get it.'* He knew where he could hide it in

the house so he could easily grab it when they cut the cake or whatever dessert was served. Before his shower he would have time to decorate plain wrapping paper with markers, art supplies Grandma always kept for the boys. And he would make a card. There was time. Grandma and Grandpa had only one bathroom with only one shower in their old-fashioned house and Charles would take a while ... *'like he always does.'*

When the boys came downstairs and entered the living room at exactly 4:45, by Charles' wristwatch, they found Grandma, Grandpa, Mrs. Sullivan, and Pat all gathered around not one but two tables. On one table were the appetizers, pitchers of sweet tea, lemonade, cups, plates, napkins, small forks, and many kinds of appetizers. On the other was a pretty blue bow.

"Come in! Come in!" Mrs. Sullivan greeted them.

"Look how clean these guys are. Good job, boys," Grandma said, nodding and smiling.

"Two tables?" Max asked.

"Yes, isn't the new end table beautiful? It was a gift from Mrs. Sullivan and Pat to us," Grandma said. "Pat made it."

"Come here and look," Pat said. "See? There's the heartwood."

"Wow. Neat," said Charles.

Max touched its silky surface. It had been sanded many times and treated with varnish. "It's amazing. This is the secret part of a tree we never see while it's alive."

"Right," said Pat. "We never see a tree's heart until it has been broken open, but it's there. Maybe, by making these tables, people will see and learn more about trees."

"Pat and I wanted your grandparents to have it. A gift from us for all the many times they've been good to us . . . using the garden and, well, in other ways, too," Mrs. Sullivan said.

"Really? Neat," said Max. He just wanted to look at it, but he was starving.

As if she heard Max's stomach growl, Grandma said, "There will be plenty of time for looking at the table. Now is the time to enjoy some appetizers."

Max and Charles turned their attention from the new table to the coffee table. Besides Grandma's standard appetizers — crackers, cheddar cheese, radishes, homemade pickled beets, and her famous bread-and-butter pickles — there were . . .

"These are Greek meatballs. We call them *keftedes*. Here, this is something you probably know: grape leaves filled with meat. Over here are some Greek olives. And here, something else you may have had: spinach pie, or in Greek we call it *spanakopita*."

"Oh, wow!"

Both Charles and Max began taking one of each.

"A feast," Grandpa said.

Dinner was one of Grandma's standards: a dinner all of Max and Charles' best friends liked to have when they came over: Great-Grandmother's recipe for German potato salad, hot pickled purple cabbage, sliced ham, and the famous "green mold." When others at school heard about a meal with green mold, they frowned and some held their noses. "Yucky!" they whispered. "What a weird Grandma. What a witch-like cook to serve green mold at a special meal." But green mold was actually a code name for a dessert made with lime and lemon Jell-O, crushed pineapple, chopped pecans, and a little cottage cheese.

"Pat, being the good Irish cook he is, has added to the meal, too," Grandma said. "These are his own strawberry/raspberry scones made from berries he picked here last year."

It all tasted great to Charles and Max.

Then dessert.

Mrs. Sullivan had prepared at home, then added finishing touches in Grandma's kitchen, little balls of dough, deep-fried and then soaked in a warm honey sauce.

"Very yummy! What are they called?" Max asked.

"Are you ready? I'll say it slowly," said Mrs. Sullivan.

"Here, I have a pad and pen." Pat pulled them from his shirt pocket.

"A good team," Grandma said.

"Here goes," said Mrs. Sullivan. "*Loukoumades.*"

"I'll have to practice saying it," said Max. He popped one into his mouth.

"Oh yum!"

"Like fried dough but as light and airy as cotton candy, only more yummy!" said Charles.

When the loukoumades were almost gone, Grandma went into the kitchen. A few moments later she returned with homemade meringues, each filled with scoops of vanilla ice cream and covered with warm fudge sauce. In one, the biggest, Grandma had placed a lit candle. Everyone sang to Mrs. Sullivan, "Happy Birthday to you."

"Oh, thank you. Thank you so much," said Mrs. Sullivan. She was weepy-happy and had to wipe her eyes.

"The pleasure is ours," Grandma said.

Grandpa gave his traditional thumbs up.

"Oh," said Max. "Be right back." He scurried from the table, went to where he had hidden his gift, and was back in a minute. "Here, for you," he said shyly to Mrs. Sullivan.

"A present? Oh, Max, how sweet," she said. "But you didn't know it was my birthday until late this afternoon."

"Oh, I ah . . . Well, I had something I made today. . . when I heard it was your birthday, well . . . and because Charles was in the shower first, I had time to wrap it for you. I hope you like it."

"I'm sure I will," said Mrs. Sullivan. First she looked at the homemade card. "Ah, Max, very kind. My favorite: a hummingbird at a flower." Then she examined the wrapping paper. "And is that me trying to cast a fishing line at the pond today? You did a great job. It looks almost as if you were spying on me."

Max kicked Charles under the table; gave him the "don't you dare tell her" look.

"A homemade card and paper, how creative," Mrs. Sullivan said. She passed both to Pat to see. He showed Grandpa and Grandma.

Meanwhile, Charles looked glum. He wished he had thought to make Mrs. Sullivan a card. *'And a present? Wow! Max really raised the bar on me this time.'*

While everyone looked at paper and card, Grandma smiled her "proud of you smile" at Max, and Pat gave him a high-five. When Grandpa saw the fly-casting wrapping paper, he examined it, even put on his reading glasses. "Hmmm," was all he said, but he smiled.

Mrs. Sullivan opened the box and looked it.

"It's pretty fragile," Max said. "You may want to wait a few days until it really has a chance to dry. Can you see it?"

"I think I can."

"Here," said Pat. He pulled a little flashlight from one of his pockets, turned it on and handed it to her.

"Oh, my, Max. Did you really make it?"

"Yes, ma'am."

"It's grand," Mrs. Sullivan said to him and the others. "Max made a little house out of stones, sticks, and, am I right, clay?"

"Yes, ma'am, clay from under the stream bank. The stones and sticks are from the stream, too. It's the same type of clay the ancient tribes used who camped here. The kind Grandpa finds in the garden. But I didn't mix it with soapstone. It's on a piece of birch bark to make it easier to carry."

"Wonderful. Very creative. I'll put it on a special shelf I have at home." Mrs. Sullivan handed the box around so Pat and the others could see and opened her arms to Max. "May I give you a thank-you hug?" she asked.

"Sure," Max said.

Charles watched, feeling sorrier and sorrier he didn't have anything to give.

"I have something for you, too," Pat said. "Actually, if it wasn't for our good friends here," he nodded to Grandpa and Grandma, "I wouldn't have it . . . so in a way it's from all of us." Grandma reached into the big pocket of her apron and pulled out a small wrapped present, and Pat handed it to his birthday-wife. "Happy Birthday to my one and only Pope-ee." He gave her a quick kiss on the cheek.

"Oh my," said Mrs. Sullivan.

Then she opened the box. It was a ring box. And there inside was a perfect arrowhead carved out of white quartz. A thin silver thread was around it twice, near its tip and middle. On its back was a silver clasp so it could be worn as jewelry.

"I'm speechless," said Mrs. Sullivan. Her eyes were a bit watery. "But tell me the story."

"Well," said Pat, "it came from the garden. No, I didn't find it. The master of all arrowhead hunters did. Then he cleaned it up and when I saw it, I asked if I could buy it."

"But no," said Grandma. "We knew he wanted to give it to you. And see," she pulled back her apron. Near the collar of her shirt she wore one just like it. "I showed mine to Pat. Grandpa gave me this one a long time ago, back when we were just dating."

"I told Pat where I had gone to have it made into a pin, actually to a great pal of mine, a jeweler. Pat took it to him," said Grandpa.

"Oh, my goodness. It is so beautiful. What a story, and, oh my, I'm already thinking how I can incorporate this into my Native American history unit which I'll be teaching next fall. Oh, thank you so much. All of you." Mrs. Sullivan got up and gave Pat a cheek kiss and then one for Grandma; lastly Grandpa, who, being Grandpa, made a crow caw noise. They all laughed.

"What a wonderful birthday I'm having," Mrs. Sullivan said.

Just then the phone rang. Grandma hurried to get it. The others chatted, looked at the presents, and the table.

Grandma returned in minutes.

"Fred and company are home. He said give them about 30 minutes, then please come up and visit," she said to Pat and Mrs. Sullivan.

"Oh, wonderful! Perfect. What a wonderful, wonderful birthday," said Mrs. Sullivan, beaming. "We'll help you clean the dishes and then we'll visit them."

"You'll do no such thing. I have two grandsons to help me. Then . . ."

"And then, boys, you better head to the campsite so you will be ready to start on our next adventure . . . waiting and finding out who's been stealing my prize trout," Grandpa said.

'*Oh, oh, oh,*' thought Max. The "adventure" he'd been dreading all day was about to begin.

Chapter 11

To Catch a Thief You Need . . .

With Fitz as their designated guard dog trotting beside them, Max and Charles were walking up the cool shady path by the fish pools to their campsite.

"What's with you?" Max asked. "I mean besides the obvious . . . sitting, waiting for some fish robber to appear tonight and what might happen next?"

"Yeah well, yeah, that's the obvious. The $1 + 1 + 1 + 1 = ?$ equation, or in literary terms, Max + Charles + Fitzgerald + robber = the Great Unknown. Yep, that's been a problem I've been contemplating, calculating, for hours now. But since Mrs. Sullivan's birthday party, I've had another troublesome problem. What can I find and give her as a birthday present? You had a gift, lucky you. And you had plenty of extra time to make it look special, but me . . . I mean really, Max, there I was, the only one in the room without some gift for her. I feel like mud. You know what I mean? So what's a good solution? Or is the problem unsolvable?"

"My brother the math whiz. OK, Charles, be creative. It's not what you give to her, it's that you *want* to give her something and whatever the something is will be fine. It means you want to please her. Mrs. Sullivan is not someone who judges a gift by some money-expense system."

"Yeah, true. You're right. But what?"

"Ah, how about something special to nibble on, growing near here, and how about something that smells really sweet growing . . ." Max said in his big brother way. He already knew what he'd give Mrs. Sullivan if he were Charles.

"You're making a riddle. OK, I like riddles. Ah, umm . . . " Charles was thinking.

Both boys and Fitzgerald stopped walking. They were standing between the Big Spring and the Little Stream.

Max stroked Fitzgerald's silky head. In the marsh to their right, a chorus of bullfrogs had started to warm up. The evening was satiny soft, and the fragrance coming from the hedge of wild roses, blooming between where they stood and their campsite, surrounded them like fog.

"Oh!" Charles said, as if waking from a dream.

"Something to nibble on could be mint or watercress!"

"Or both."

"Or both. But I don't have Grandpa's penknife to cut the roots away from the cress, and a bouquet with white wet roots hanging down is not very attractive. But mint, yep. Here's the patch."

"Exactly," Max said.

"A bouquet of mint." Charles went down on his knees in the dewy wet grass. He snapped the long stems of peppermint, adding spearmint, and orange mint for variety. In minutes he held a fistful of long stems topped by the rough dark leaves. "But I want to give her something more." He was quiet for a moment, listening to the bullfrogs' "brr-rumping" baritones and basses. He blew out a long cleansing breath, then slowly sucked in more and more of the sweet wild perfume. Mouth open, looking like a fish out of water, eyes widening, he stared at Max. "A bouquet of wild roses. Yeah, perfect. Will you help me?"

"I'll hold the mint while you gather your roses," Max said. He was wise to the hazards of briars in rose bushes.

'Yes,' Charles thought, 'a perfect gift showing an effort had been made.' He had never picked delicate wild rose petals. With no knife, no scissors, he had to find the least thorny places. Not easy. Gently snapping stems without having the entire bloom lose its petals. "Ouch. Oooch. Oh, darn! This really pretty one just went all naked on me."

"Don't pick the ones blooming. Pick the buds. Here, maybe this will help." Max handed Charles one of the small white quartz stones he'd found earlier at the Big Stream. This one had a worked sharp edge but no point. Max paused before handing it to Charles, wondering, 'Could it be an arrowhead? Grandpa said some little ones were made. They're called bird points. But this one is pointless. Ugh, pun. Maybe over hundreds of years, the point broke off.'

"Here, Charles," he said, "but when you're done, give it back. I want to show it to Grandpa."

Sawing stems with the sharp stone edge helped. Charles' fingers still felt itchy from the tiny prickling thorns, but stems were cut quicker, and by choosing buds over blooms, fewer petals fell. He had his bouquet of white and pink wild roses in about ten minutes.

"Now what?"

"I'll take Fitz and go to the camp. You take your gifts to Mrs. Sullivan. I'm sure Mom is still chatting away with her. But hurry, I'd really rather not be alone if the robber comes. Oh, and Charles, I'll hand you back the mint when you return to me that bird point you used for sawing the rose stems. I saw you pocket it," Max said.

"Oops, sorry," Charles said. He dug the quartz stone out of his "prized possessions" pocket. "I forgot."

Max took the stone and pushed it as far as he could into his deepest jeans pocket. He handed the mint to Charles. "Quick, easy steps, don't run, because if you run you could still lose your petals."

"OK. I hear you. Thanks, Max. You really can be a helpful big brother."

"Don't get mushy on me, Charles."

Charles headed towards their home. As he walked, he thought, *'I almost had a bird point. Oh, well, that really wouldn't have been honest. All this robber stuff. I'm fighting off the urge to take what's not mine. Not good.'*

Meanwhile, Max walked towards the campsite with Fitzgerald hugging his legs, sniffing his feet, wagging her plumb-feathered tail, acting like he was the best friend she'd ever had in all the world.

"You like it out here with me, don't you, Fitz? Sweet gal, I feel lots better with you near," said Max.

Away from the trout pools and Big Spring, the air was warmer. Standing in the open pasture, it was much lighter than by the shaded pools. It wasn't sunset yet.

Before Max, Charles, and Fitz had started "up to camp," Grandpa had consulted his Farmer's Almanac. "Sunrise this morning was officially at 6:08. Sunset will be, according to this wise resource, exactly at 8:00. 'Course, some clouds have moved in since this afternoon. It could get dark earlier."

Max knew when Charles went to give Mrs. Sullivan his presents, it was 7:32 p.m. He hoped Charles would hurry back.

Charles did. Within ten minutes he was running full gallop. By 7:42 he stood panting by Max's side. "You been in camp yet?"

"No, wanted to wait for you."

"Well, let's go then."

The boys and Fitzgerald walked the few yards to the grove of cedars and bushy enclosing long-needled pines.

"Mrs. Sullivan like her bouquets?" Max asked.

"Yeah, too much so. She cried and gave me one of her motherly hugs. Then Mom hugged me, too. Man, I was glad Fred and Pat weren't around. I've had my share of hugs until Christmas and then some."

"Well, I'm glad you made her happy. As for the hugs, I don't think we'll be hug-free until Christmas," Max said.

"No? Why?"

"Because on August 12, you turn nine and I turn twelve."

"Oh, yeah. Shared birthdays. I guess Mom planned it so she wouldn't have to remember many different dates. Like February 13 was the day Carrie was born, on Ralph's birthday. Man, did that ever mess up his party plans."

Both boys laughed over Ralph's birthday being spent in the "Important Sibling Waiting Room" of the birthing center at their local hospital.

They stopped in mid-laugh.

Someone had been at the camp site. Someone had made changes. It was not the way it had been when they left it earlier.

Max and Charles' hearts began thumping faster than when they went running.

There, just outside the enclosure where their tent was pitched, were two short logs big enough to sit on, two lawn chairs, which looked like ones their mom and Fred had, two rubber mats to make the ground softer when placed under sleeping bags, two rolled-up sleeping bags, and two gallon-size plastic milk jugs full of water, the kind Fred and their Mom used when they went camping.

"Huh? I wonder who's been here?"

"I wonder where they are?" asked Charles.

"Right here!" A man's voice came from where their tent was set up.

Max and Charles each jumped at least twelve inches . . . straight up.

The pine boughs parted and from the tent, bent in half,

almost crawling, came one man and then another.

The boys felt instant relief.

Fitz ran to greet . . .

"Pat? Fred?"

"Hey, glad you two decided to join us. It's getting kind of late," said Fred.

"But?"

"Did you think your grandparents, Mom, or Mrs. Sullivan would let you guys face a fish robber all alone? No way!" said Fred.

"Besides, there was no way we were going to miss this kind of excitement," said Pat.

"Now, we have to get real quiet. It's almost sunset," said Fred. He sat down on one of the lawn chairs.

Pat took the other. The stumps were for the boys. Fitz saw the mats and sleeping bags, she circled and slumped on top, ready to sleep.

"Your mom and Mrs. Sullivan are having their ladies' chat. We've come down to be with you. And if takes all night, we're prepared. The ladies are having their 'girls' sleepover,' "

Fred whispered. "If you get thirsty, here's some spring water. And if you need to 'visit a tree,' well, there are plenty."

"But what if the robber is dangerous?" Max whispered. The question had been building up inside of him all day. He knew he could still act like a little boy in front of Fred. Pat and Fred both held up brightly colored, red-and-yellow horns with black rubber bulbs.

"Bike horns. They should make plenty of noise to scare

someone who is trespassing," Fred said.

"And if we need help, I have my emergency radio. I can call 911 and a few police friends of mine will be here in seconds, literally. They've just set up a radar trap at the end of the Property where the two main roads meet," Pat said with a smile.

"Ohhhh!"

"Ohhhh!"

'Hard to admit, but it sure feels good having grownups near just in case,' thought Charles.

'I wonder what Grandpa is expecting? What he knows or suspects about the robber we don't know?' Max wondered.

They all sat in silence, listening to the quiet "puff and pur-ouph" of Fitz snoring. They listened to the bullfrog chorus, now in tune, all rumbling full-bodied "brr-rump, brr-rump, brrrrr-rummpppp." On the other side of the marsh, a higher peeping sound from smaller green frogs and spring peepers.

Pink and blue sunset filled the sky, swirling colors, melting cloud shapes one into another, then deepening blues turned into purples and grays while pink blurred to red rose, mellowing, fading into murky maroons.

Then, into the rhyming, rhythmic sun-setting ease of day-falling-into-night . . . just then, before darkness:

"Rrrrrrrrrrrrrrrrrrrrr. Grr. Hissssssss! Growl." Followed by a chittering, chattering, rattling. Sounds that dinosaur experts believe some of those extinct creatures may have made.

"What!" Max and Charles eeked.

"Shh!" Pat and Fred whispered, fingers to lips.

"Look, by the Big Spring," Fred said softly. "Do you see him? He's there, come to steal one of Grandpa's beauties. But he won't be lucky tonight."

Max and Charles looked, then they saw it.

There by the Big Spring the tall, blue and gray robber stalked, closer and closer, along the bank, head down, eyes staring, body tense, ready to act. Ready to attack.

"Aah!"

"Ooo!"

"Gah!"

"Aah-ooo-gah!" Both horns blared loudly together, then two times more just to be sure the robber heard.

Fred, Pat, Max, and Charles heard a howl. It echoed through the still night and around the Big Spring like a grinding, grist-mill wheel, a sound silencing the bullfrog chorus, a sound that seemed to quiet breezes and twig-chimes, a sound that chilled. It left the two men and two boys shaking and woke the noble guard dog from her dreams.

Next there was a loud, slicing sound as six-foot wings spread open, feathers unfolding out, "ssissing, ssissing," lifting the great blue and gray heron into the air, away, away, its long bill pointing to a next destination. No, it would not stab and kill Grandpa's pet fish here, but instead fly away. Long legs were not stalking through the high grass beside the Big Spring, but positioned out behind its plump body like two flesh-covered sticks.

"The great blue heron is the trout robber," Fred said as the bird flew out of sight. "What your grandpa predicted."

Chapter 12

And in the End

After the great blue heron clicked-clicked-clattered-clacked, chattered, rattled, hissed, growled, howled one last grumbling, scowling roar; after he had flown someplace far, far away; after contacts had been made with grandparents, Mrs. Sullivan, and their Mom; after all the excitement began to ease away, Pat said:

"Anybody interested in some debriefing, decompressing, recovering conversation over a campfire's sparkle, crackle, pop, and warmth? I've got all the makings. A few bushel baskets of kindling and snappy firewood your grandpa delivered here in his cart. It was hidden from possible spying eyes in the tent under warm comforters."

"Really?" Charles asked.

"Wow!" Max said.

"Then around this campfire, a comfy hot-dog feast in

case fear has made hunger return. Also all the necessary items needed for an early midnight-snack dessert: graham crackers, king-sized marshmallows, and a twelve-pack of chocolate bars," added Fred.

"S'mores!" both boys yelled.

"Methinks our lads have pronounced this idea good," Pat laughed, using a royal accent.

Then, from Fred:

"Take flashlights bright.
You'll find them there
Inside your tent on comforters.
Quickly, now, as every moment
Shadows grow darker,
For night begins.
Bring back long sticks,
We'll need ten:
Four for hot dogs,
Four for s'mores.
Two for Fitz to fetch
Or chew.
To find them
Walk towards the house ten
Times ten
Leapfrog footsteps,
To where
Great tall oaks have grown
But winter's storm
Whirled, blew twigs and branches
Now are blown down
Resting broken on the ground.

Gusty winds:

Nature the true

Pruner."

Crafting directions to the boys in free form, rhyming-sometimes, free verse, poetic form, Fred took a bow.

Pat and the boys applauded.

"If I had one on my head, I'd tip my hat to these poetic directions. What an excellent parody of comic speeches written by the famous bard, William Shakespeare," Pat said, chuckling.

"Oh, it was my attempt to not be verbally outdone by you, Pat, my wordsmith friend," Fred said. Both men shook hands.

"OK, without trying poetry, we're off to do what you've asked," Max said. He crawled away from the gathering, through the sheltering pines, and into the tent.

"Here, Charles, I have a light for you, too."

While the boys went in search of ten sticks, Pat and Fred worked together to build the campfire. Pat had been an Eagle Scout. Now, ten years later, he and Mrs. Sullivan spent many vacations hiking and camping. Both loved listening to campfires "singing" their own smoky songs. They loved telling tales to each other, some about growing up, some silly ones made from their imaginations.

Meanwhile, Charles and Max crept with their flashlights as the world around them grew darker and darker. Soon they found the place where March winds had been the natural pruners of the oaks. They found the ten sticks they needed, "plus two more, just in case," Charles said.

Soon they were back at camp: two boys, two men, and

their trusting pet.

"In school we get tests with fill-in-the-blanks. I think there are blanks to be filled in about what has happened today and tonight," Max said.

Pat took out a baggie filled with hot dogs and passed it to Fred, who took out one and passed the bag to Max who took out three: "One for Charles, one for Fitz, one for me," he said, handing the bag back to Pat.

"Well, in school, as I know from living these wonderful five years married to a third-grade teacher, I've learned for each test a teacher gives, there's an answer sheet. It's a pretty easy test to mark and grade," Pat said in his slow, thoughtful, storyteller way. "But you see, in this case the test was multiple choice, and as you know, sometimes the answers on those tests read: 1) Yes 2) No 3) N/A 4) Unknown (or not enough information shown). Right?"

"Mostly," Charles said, thinking of multiple-choice tests he had known and loved, or not.

"Pretty much. I really don't care for either one," said Max. "My favorites are essays. I have time to develop my answer. I prefer essay tests when a yes/no doesn't allow for what Grandpa would probably call 'wiggle room.'"

"Very true," Pat said.

"Agreed," said Fred.

"All your grandpa knew this morning was that several of his prize trout were missing, he had seen a great blue heron stalking at the farm pond earlier this week, and great blue herons are smart, territorial birds particularly fond of a shallow pool, spring, or pond. He told his theory to Mrs. Sullivan and me as we were walking back from the garden after her casting lesson," Pat said.

"And Grandpa and Grandma, being Grandpa and Grandma, would never have let either of you boys enter into a 'danger zone' alone," Fred said. "But both are believers of experience learning, rather than a simple telling or watching a 60-minute documentary on TV with thirty minutes devoted to commercials."

"Hands-on learning. Mrs. Sullivan and I are strong believers in it, too," said Pat. "When we heard the 'plan' your grandparents were cooking up to have you two wait tonight and hopefully meet Mr. Heron, which could sadly end with another swallowed trout, we told your grandparents: 'Count us in!' Oh, we had already planned on having dinner here. And it *is* really Mrs. Sullivan's birthday . . ."

"Your mother and I really *did* have a sudden change of plans," continued Fred. "We only had a few wonderful hours to see our dear friend, who *really* was returning from France and on her way to Alaska. There was a weather delay in the Midwest, so she was stuck here. And stuck meant time to hang out with us and to meet baby Carrie at BWI Airport. *And* it was great to see her and let her hold Carrie (not much of a baby anymore, but still a wee little one) for the very first time. Our next chance to see her will be maybe in six months, maybe another year. She's a doctor, did you know? She works for the wonderful organization called Doctors Without Borders. It was started in 1971. Many people doing good to help others around the world. She travels to wherever they need her."

Pat picked up the narrative. "Anyway, Fred and I knew the gals would need gal talk. We suspected you two would be totally freaked here alone. So, it was decided, just like we said: the gals would enjoy their talking sleepover. And we guys would join with you guys for a campout and hopefully catch or scare away a fish robber."

"It all worked. And with this campfire . . ." Charles stopped. "I mean, it's fun and it would not have been fun. The noise the great blue heron made . . . I mean . . ."

"Yeah, it was the scariest thing I ever heard," Max said.

The men and boys ate their hot dogs and were onto the s'mores when the subject came up of what could be done to keep the blue heron out of the spring.

"I've been doing some research. I need to discuss it with your grandpa, but there are several things we could do that would be considered a 'natural' solution," Pat said. "One seems to fit your grandpa's style: string fishing line back and forth just under the water. The other, which I happen to like and which I'd love to work on: gather stones and place them, like a border, all the way around the spring. I hear great blue herons don't like to stalk where they might get pebbles between their toes."

"Oh, I like the pebble idea. What do you think, Fred?" asked a marshmallow-gooey Charles.

"I like it. But Grandpa will have the final say."

"But if we did do the pebbles, could we all work on it? I mean like a team? Like we did today? Because today it felt like, all day, like we were a team. And it didn't matter how old we were or what our skills might be . . . It was like we were all equal. It wasn't like kids against adults. Or adults telling kids what to do." Max paused to catch his breath. "I mean, sometimes it felt like that, for a little while, maybe, but now, when you tell us all the planning and all the reasons and all the working to make things better for each other . . . I mean, it has been a great day. Count me in to do whatever I can."

"Meee tooo," said a sticky Charles.

"OK, guys. We'll see what Grandpa and the women say, but sounds good to me. How about to you, Fred?"

"Count me in. I say YES to intergenerational teams. I like it. But now, guys, it's late. And I have my 'Dad role' on this team, which means one more marshmallow, then clean up as best you can, crawl in your tent, wrap a comforter around you, and go to sleep." He looked at his watch. "It's almost 10:00. It has been, for some . . . for two boys I know, who were up at sunrise, a very long day."

"I'll warm a pot of water over the fire," said Pat. He pulled a two-quart pot from his pack. "Here's soap and a cloth."

Max and Charles each picked one last marshmallow, placed it on their sticks and held it over the campfire. When both marshmallows were simmering flames, they lifted them high, two tiny torches against the black night sky.

"Charles," Max said, "by the flame of this marshmallow torch I vow to be a better team brother to you."

"Max," said Charles, "by the flame of this marshmallow torch I vow to be a better team brother to you."

Then on a "one, two, three," they blew out the glowing marshmallows together. And as soon as the soft, sticky, gooey delight cooled, again on a "one, two, three," they ate the marshmallows at the same time, crossed their sticks in the air and said:

"All Done."

Epilogue

Today, as was the way when I was a child, a journey over a hilly, curving road into Caves Valley, Maryland, can still be taken. Thanks to the Valleys Planning Council, woodlands and farmlands have been saved from large developments.

As you travel away from Baltimore City into Baltimore County, two roads intersect and you must stop at a four-way stop sign. At this corner, on your right, begins the Property. If you arrive there in early spring, thousands of blooming daffodils, jonquils, and narcissus fill lowlands surrounding tiny streams. They were planted by my grandfather, Simeon, sometime around 1920. If you happen to arrive in early May and take no turns, but continue driving straight, you enter a tunnel of catawba trees with large white blossoms; some of the trees are old, crooked, and worn, some younger and taller. Their spicy scent blends with the yellow and white blooms on honeysuckle vines, and prickly wild briar rose. This blended fragrance is a perfume so intense it will remain in your memory always.

The fish pools in this story were, for over twenty years, a nine-month "home" for brook trout. Here about 1,500 a year grew from three-inch fingerlings into ten- to seventeen-inch adults. Sadly, these pools are no longer functioning. They await someone who may wish to raise these fragile, "must have pure cold spring water" fish once again. Thanks to all who belonged to the Maryland Fly Anglers club, thousands of trout thrived in these clean, protected pools and were safely delivered to "fly fishing only," "fish for fun," "catch and release" streams. One was Hunting Creek, which flows through Catoctin State Park and the Presidents' retreat, Camp David, in western Maryland. These trout were fed twice a day by my Mom, Dad, myself, my children, and friends of our family.

The Big Spring and little streams beside it are filled with tangy watercress and bubbles. Mint grows in the long grass, and water skimmers (or water spiders) skate across the mirror-smooth surface. Crayfish challenge with snapping claws held in aggressive position. Nearby, the grove of oaks stands, though storms have reduced their numbers. The covered spring continues to be a favored home for red salamanders. The Grove of moss and stone remains undisturbed.

The Big Stream where "Max" and "Charles" went for a swim waits for other children to play there, where tiny minnows hide in the shadows of deeper pools. The cool waters flow through shallows, only inches above pink, brown, and white quartz stones where spears, perfect arrowheads and points can be found. Under its banks, there is gray clay for making little cabins or soapstone pottery as once was made by ancient Native American tribes.

The garden is gone, but the farm pond remains shadowed by tall cattails. And here on warm spring and summer nights, one can hear bullfrogs singing competition choruses.

At sunrise, or just before sunset, the great blue heron stalks where there are fish, frogs, and other prey. This tall heron is a good hunter, waiting for the moment, the chance . . . then its long, great beak opens, then snaps, swallowing whole its dinner. It clicks-chatters and when disturbed, hisses, growls, howls increasingly loud; one can only imagine its roar as something prehistoric dinosaurs may have made.

Many generations of children in our family have learned through play, passing down stories about respect, value, and the importance of educating others about about care of our environment. Raised in enchanted nature, young adults continue to describe the importance of places where their imaginations were nurtured by wonderment.

Susan Yaruta-Young
May 23, 2015

CPSIA information can be obtained
at www.ICGtesting.com
Printed in the USA
BVHW080428151218
535696BV00001B/119/P

9 781944 962401